IT'S ALIVE! IT'S ALIVE!

GOOSEBUMPS®

Also available as ebooks

ALSO AVAILABLE:

IT'S ALIVE! IT'S ALIVE!

R.L. STINE

SCHOLASTIC INC.

Goosebumps book series created by Parachute Press, Inc.
Copyright © 2019 by Scholastic Inc.

All rights reserved. Published by Scholastic Inc., *Publishers since 1920.* SCHOLASTIC, GOOSEBUMPS, GOOSEBUMPS HORRORLAND, and associated logos are trademarks and/or registered trademarks of Scholastic Inc.

ISBN 978-1-338-22303-3

10 9 8 7 6 5 4 3 2 1   19 20 21 22 23

Printed in the U.S.A.   40
First printing 2019

SLAPPY HERE, EVERYONE.

Welcome to *SlappyWorld*.

Yes, it's Slappy's world—You're only screaming in it! Hahahaha!

Does everyone think I'm as wonderful as I know I am? I only wish I had *two* mouths. Then I could *kiss* myself! Hahaha!

But I don't like to brag. It gets in the way of me telling you how awesome I am.

Everyone loves Slappy. Even the termites inside my head think I'm delicious! Hahahaha.

Some people think I got to be a big movie star because of my looks. And guess what—they're *right*! Hahahaha!

But I play well with others. I like to share. I like to share scary stories that will make you *scream*!

Like this one. It's about a girl named Livvy Jones and her friend Gates. They're on the Robotics Team at school. They have fun building a robot—until the robot goes rogue. It starts

1

to act in dangerous ways, ways that Livvy and Gates can't control.

Can a robot come to life on its own?

The answer may surprise you.

Go ahead. Start reading. I call this story *It's Alive! It's Alive!*

It's another one of my frightening tales from *SlappyWorld*.

"I dreamed our robot came alive and went berserk," I told Gates Warwas. We were walking home from school, and of course, we were talking about Robotics. Because we are obsessed.

A yellow school bus rolled by, and some kids shouted at us from the windows. I waved at them, but I didn't bother to see who they were. I was busy telling Gates about my dream.

My name is Livvy Jones. I'm twelve, and I have very real, very exciting dreams, and in the morning, I remember every single one of them. I think it's good to tell people your dreams because they can help you figure out what they mean.

So I told Gates my dream. "The robot ran away, and I chased after it. But it was too fast for me. It ran to a big parking lot and it began picking up cars. It lifted them high in the air, then smashed them to the pavement."

Gates had a thoughtful look on his face. Of course, he always has a thoughtful look on his face. That's Gates's thing. He's quiet and he's thoughtful. His dark eyes gazed straight ahead, and he kept nodding thoughtfully as he listened to me.

"The robot smashed one car after another. It was a very noisy dream," I said. "I think all the crashing and smashing is what woke me. I sat straight up in bed and I was shaking. The dream was so real."

We crossed the street. Gates continued to look thoughtful.

"So? What do you think it means?" I said.

He scratched his head. He has curly black hair that pops straight up. He can't keep it down. It's like it's alive.

We turned and cut through the Murphys' backyard. They probably wouldn't like our shortcut through their yard every afternoon, but they're never home. My house is three houses down.

"I think it means that we shouldn't have made our robot look so human," Gates said finally.

"Huh? What do you mean?"

"Everyone else is building robots that look like machines," he continued. "But we built ours to look like a girl. And I think maybe that's what is freaking you out. We built a girl. It's too real."

"But I love Francine," I said.

Gates rolled his eyes. "We can't call a robot Francine. No way."

"Why not?"

4

"Because you can't. You just can't have a robot named Francine."

I gave him a playful shove. "She is my idea and I get to name her."

"No way, Livvy," Gates whined. "Francine. Francine the Robot. It's too . . . embarrassing." He crossed his arms in front of his chest. "I'm going to talk to Coach Teague about it. Seriously."

Harrison Teague is the coach of our Robotics Team. He is a good guy. And he keeps us psyched. He's keeping us pumped up and eager to beat Swanson Academy in the Springdale Robotics Meet this year. Swanson Academy is where all the rich kids go. They're our rival, our enemy school. In football, in basketball—in *everything*.

Teague doesn't know that much about Robotics. He admits it himself. I mean, he's the girls' basketball coach, and the school gave him the Robotics Team to coach in his spare time. They sort of forced it on him.

I stopped outside my family's garage. I lowered my backpack to the driveway. "Listen, Gates, we can't argue about the robot's name now. We are so close to finishing her. We just have a few tweaks to make on the programming. This is no time to fight."

He shrugged. "You're right. I think she's ready for us to test some of her skills this afternoon." He pumped a fist above his head. "This is exciting, Livvy."

5

It *was* exciting. Gates and I had been building the robot in my garage for months. Programming her memory module took weeks and weeks.

And now we were finally about to see what she could do.

My family has a white-shingled, two-car garage. But my parents never put their cars in it. They always park them in the driveway. That gave Gates and me the perfect workshop to build Francine.

I bent down and grabbed the door on the left. Gates helped me and we both pushed the door up.

"Let's see what we have here," Gates said, rubbing his hands together like a mad scientist in a horror movie. "How is our little experiment?"

We both stopped. We both stared. We both uttered startled cries.

"The robot . . ." I murmured. "She's GONE!"

What was the first thing I thought of?

My dream, of course.

Once again, I saw the robot running down the street. Picking up cars. Smashing them on the pavement.

Is that what happened here? Did my dream come true? Did Francine run away?

Of course not.

She couldn't walk quickly or very far. And she definitely wasn't programmed to open the garage door and then close it again.

Gates and I stood in the center of the garage, staring at the spot where the robot should have been.

"Have we been robbed?" Gates said finally. His voice came out tiny and a little bit shaky.

I opened my mouth to reply, but stopped when I heard laughter.

"Whoa." I spun around to the open door.

Gates sighed. "I recognize that laugh."

So did I.

We both dove out of the garage—and saw Chaz Fremont on the patio. He stood there laughing his hee-haw donkey laugh with one arm around Francine.

Yes. He had Francine.

He had been hiding behind the garage, waiting for us. Waiting to give Gates and me a little scare. Because Chaz loves to torture us and torment us and tease us and bully us and give us a hard time.

He's not our favorite dude.

Also, I have to mention this—Chaz doesn't go to Springdale Middle School like Gates and me. He goes to Swanson Academy.

And I have to tell you one more thing about Chaz, who has short, spiky red hair and freckles on his big round face, and tiny blue eyes that look like bird eyes, and is big and hulky and works out a lot. He's the captain of the Swanson Academy Robotics Team, which beats us at the meet every year. Because Chaz is a *genius* robot builder.

I don't like him, but I have to say that to be fair.

"What are you doing with Francine?" I demanded.

Chaz's mouth dropped open. "Francine? You can't call a robot Francine. I think you should call it Livvy Two, because it looks just like you, except a lot cuter. Haha."

"You're not funny," I said. "Give us back our robot."

"Sure. You can have it." He slid his arm off Francine's shoulders and took a few steps back. "I was just pulling your chain. I forgot you don't have a sense of humor."

"You're about as funny as pig vomit," Gates said.

"Oh, good one," Chaz replied. "Did you just make that up?"

Gates blushed. He blushes easily, and Chaz always knows how to make him blush.

Gates and I lifted our robot off the patio stones and began carrying her into the garage. She weighed a ton. We used molded sheet metal for the body. And the computer that held all the memory modules was also heavy.

Chaz followed us, cracking his knuckles in front of him as he walked, one of his gross habits. "What does it do?" he asked. "Wave bye-bye? Or was that too hard for you to program?"

"Why would we tell you?" I shot back. "You're the enemy, remember?"

"I'm the frenemy," Chaz said. "Remember? Robotics is all about *cooperatition.*"

That's a word some Robotics coach made up somewhere. A combination of *cooperation* and *competition.* It means we cooperate and compete at the same time. "Robotics is the most friendly competition." That's what Coach Teague keeps reminding us all the time.

9

Chaz picked up a pair of hedge clippers from a shelf and pretended to cut Francine's head off. "Your robot is so totally old-school," he said. "Like an old sci-fi movie."

"Old-school enough to beat your robot," Gates told him.

"I don't think so," Chaz replied. "At Swanson, we're all building sports robots this year. I built a basketball robot. It can toss up three-point shots on any court without missing a single one."

He pretended to fire off a jump shot. "How can you beat that? No one can. They should just cancel the contest and give me the trophy today."

"At least you don't brag a lot," Gates said.

And then I burst out and told Chaz what our robot could do. I don't know why I did it. It was supposed to be a secret. But since he was standing there bragging about his robot, I decided I should brag about Francine.

"On the Springdale team, we're all building construction robots," I said. "We programmed Francine to construct an omelet."

Chaz laughed. "Haha. Does she also lay the eggs?"

"Want to try her?" I said. "We'll show you what she can do. She's a genius with her hands. You won't be laughing. You'll be home programming your robot to clap for ours."

Gates patted me on the shoulder. "Nice one,

Livvy. But we haven't really finished her yet, remember?"

"Show me something," Chaz insisted. "Go ahead. Show me what she can do. I bet she can't even crack an egg."

"Of course she can crack an egg," I said. "She can crack a dozen eggs perfectly." I should have just shut up. But Chaz always puts me in a state.

And that's how we ended up with Francine in the kitchen. No one was home. My mom was still at work at her science lab. I pulled out a large bowl and filled it with eggs from the fridge.

We carried the bowl to the table. Gates activated the robot and the remote control. Then we attached the metal squeezer hands onto the robot's arms.

Chaz hee-hawed. "No way, dudes. No way this robot will pick up an egg and crack it, then pick up another egg and crack it. You don't have the skills. We're talking major fail here."

"We're talking major victory over you," I said. I nodded to Gates. He flicked the power switch and pushed some buttons on the remote to get Francine moving.

The robot lowered her head, then raised it. That was the signal that she was powered up and ready. The three of us huddled around it, our eyes on the robot hand as the arm slowly slid up. Then slowly lowered itself.

The squeezer claw moved in and out, as if practicing. The arm moved slowly down . . . slowly . . .

. . . *and the robot claw grabbed Chaz's hand and clamped shut on it hard.*

"Hey—!" He let out a startled cry. "Get it off me!"

I saw the metal prongs of the hand tighten, pressing into Chaz's skin.

"Owwwwww!" A howl of pain escaped his throat. *"Owwwww.* My hand! My hand! *It's breaking my hand!"*

I turned to Gates. "We have to stop it!"

Gates's eyes were bulging. His mouth hung open. Frozen in horror, we both watched as the metal prongs dug deeper into Chaz's hand.

Chaz let out another scream of pain. And then I shuddered and shut my eyes—when I heard a loud, sick **CRRRAAAAAACK.**

I took a deep breath. Then I grabbed the robot's claw with my right hand and Chaz's hand with my left. He was howling like a hurt dog, his eyes shut tight.

I gave a sharp tug and Francine's prongs opened. Chaz pulled away and staggered toward the wall, waving his hurt hand above his head. Bright red blood trickled onto the kitchen floor.

"Is it broken?" I cried. "Is it?"

Chaz was panting, doing a dance of pain, still waving the hand. I saw his fingers move. "Not . . . broken," he choked out. "Just a deep cut."

Gates disappeared into the hall. A few seconds later, he returned carrying bandages. We wrapped Chaz's hand up tightly. Actually, it wasn't a bad cut. The prongs that punctured the skin were small.

Holding his arm, Chaz backed away from us. He narrowed his eyes and scowled at us both. "You did this deliberately," he muttered.

"No way," I said.

"We didn't program Francine to squeeze anyone's hand," Gates added.

"Yes you did," Chaz said, rubbing his bad hand with his good one. "I know you did."

"You've got to believe us—" I started.

But to my surprise, Francine suddenly began to move. She tossed back her head, her mouth slid open. And she let out a noise that sounded a lot like laughter.

"Urk! Urk! Urk!"

"She's laughing at me!" Chaz screamed. "What is your *problem*? You two idiots programmed this ugly thing to laugh at me!"

"No. I swear—!" I started. "We didn't."

Gates raised his right hand. "I swear. We never did. We don't know how to do that, Chaz."

"Urk! Urk! Urk!"

The robot uttered its metallic laugh again.

Chaz headed to the kitchen door. His face was red. His whole face was twisted in anger. He waved a finger at us. "I'll get you back."

I started after him. "Chaz—listen. You've got to believe us. I'm so sorry about your hand. And—"

"Urk! Urk! Urk!"

Chaz's face darkened to purple. "I'll get even," he said through clenched teeth. "Don't worry. I know how."

He spun away and darted outside. Gates and I

14

watched him run down the driveway, holding his bandaged hand.

We were silent for a long moment. Both of us thinking hard. Then I turned to Gates. "We didn't program Francine to do *any* of that. What's going on?"

Gates ran his fingers through his curly black hair. It bounced under his touch and popped up in all directions. His hair really does look as if it's alive.

He had a thoughtful gaze as he stared at me with those dark eyes. "I don't get it," he said finally.

Not a very helpful answer.

"Let's try the egg thing again," I said.

He lowered his eyes to the bowl of eggs. "Are you serious?"

"Sure," I said. "Maybe Francine is warmed up now. Maybe this time it will work."

"She just squeezed Chaz's hand like it was a tomato," Gates said. "I don't think—"

"We spent weeks programming the egg skill. It's got to work. Francine just didn't like Chaz," I joked.

Gates laughed. "Okay. Let's try it. But don't put your hand too close to her."

I turned Francine toward the kitchen counter and slid the bowl of eggs in front of her. I checked to make sure the squeezer hand with its long prongs was on tightly.

"Go ahead. Activate her," Gates said. He took a few steps back. Coward.

Before I could push the ON button, Mrs. Bernard walked into the kitchen. She blinked a few times. "You brought that machine into the house? What are you doing with those eggs?"

Mrs. Bernard is our housekeeper and babysitter. She's pretty old, about sixty, I think. She has short white curls on her head. Twinkly blue eyes. Her face is always pink, as if she's excited. She's very sweet and hardworking and kind, but I've never seen her smile.

She wears little square eyeglasses, which are always sliding down her nose. She's shorter than Gates and me, and we're only twelve. She wears white blouses buttoned to the neck and dark gray skirts that come down to her ankles.

"We're doing an experiment," I told her.

She frowned and shook her head. "I just cleaned the kitchen. I don't need any mess from that machine."

"It isn't a machine. It's a robot," Gates said. "We built it for our Robotics Team."

She sniffed. "Shouldn't you be doing your homework instead?"

"We won't make a mess. I promise," I said. "You can watch, too, Mrs. B."

"Francine is going to crack the eggs," Gates said. "One at a time."

Mrs. Bernard frowned again. "You built this machine to replace *me*?"

I laughed. "She can be your kitchen helper when you need to crack eggs."

She crossed her arms in front of her. "This I've got to see. And you promise—?"

"No mess," I said.

I threw the switch. The robot began to vibrate. She nodded her head, the signal that she was ready.

The three of us watched from the other side of the counter. "Come on, Francine. You can do it," I said.

The arm rose, then slowly lowered. The prongs on the hand tightened around an egg in the bowl.

I could feel my excitement growing as the hand gently lifted the egg. "Yes ... yes ... yes ..." I whispered.

"This is the way it's supposed to go," Gates murmured.

The hand slowly raised the egg. It held it for a few seconds over the countertop. Then the claw moved sharply forward—and smashed the egg hard into my forehead.

"Ohhhh." I was too startled to scream.

I heard the loud *craaack*. I stumbled back a

step. And felt the yolk ooze slowly down my nose and cheeks.

"*Urk! Urk! Urk!*"

The robot belched out its ugly laugh.

I wiped the egg yolk from my eyes with both hands. And watched as Francine raised another egg—and smashed it on top of Gates's head.

He uttered an angry cry. The egg yolk stuck to his thick hair and stayed on his head.

"Turn it off! Turn it off!" Mrs. Bernard shrieked, tossing her hands in the air. "Oh, what a mess!"

"*Urk! Urk! Urk!*"

Gates scrambled around the counter. He slid his hand to the robot's back and fumbled for the power switch.

Francine tossed an egg at the kitchen wall. It splattered with a loud *craaack*. The yolk streaked down the wallpaper. Another egg sailed into the clock over the kitchen sink. Yolk ran down the white curtains over the window.

Francine heaved another egg onto the wall.

"Turn it off! Turn it off!" Mrs. Bernard was screeching, tearing at her white hair.

And that's when my parents returned home. They stood at the kitchen door, their eyes darting over the sticky, yellow, oozing mess.

"What have you done?" Mom cried.

5

"*Urk! Urk! Urk!*"

Francine tossed back her head and uttered her ugly laugh.

"This isn't funny!" Dad cried. He stepped into the room, his eyes on the yellow glop running down the kitchen wall.

"Their machine went loopy," Mrs. Bernard said.

"I ... I don't understand," Mom stammered. "Livvy—?"

"I'll get a mop and some cloths." Mrs. Bernard scurried from the room.

"It was an experiment," Gates said.

"Our first test for the robot," I added. "But ... well ..."

Mrs. Bernard burst back in with a mop and bucket in her hands. "That machine doesn't belong in the house," she said.

Mom crossed her arms in front of her. She

20

chewed at her bottom lip. She always does that when she's tense or upset. Dad just looked confused.

"What exactly happened here?" Mom said.

"We programmed Francine to pick up eggs and crack them," I said. "But when we tried her out, she went berserk."

"She smashed eggs on Livvy and me," Gates said. He still had a puddle of yellow yolk on top of his head. "Then she began tossing eggs everywhere."

"Loopy. Just loopy," Mrs. Bernard muttered. She was leaning over the mop as she cleaned the floor.

"Are you really going to call that robot Francine?" Dad asked.

"Benjamin, that's not what we're talking about," Mom scolded. Usually, he's Ben. But she always calls him Benjamin when she's angry.

I shook my head. "I guess Gates and I messed up the programming," I said.

"First, we'll clean up the mess," Mom said. "Then we'll check her after dinner."

Mom and Dad are computer programmers. They work together in a lab downtown. They are both experts in artificial intelligence. You know. Designing brain modules that allow computers and robots to think on their own.

That's how I got interested in Robotics. My

parents talk about their work a lot. And a few times, they let Gates and me come to their lab and see the experiments they're doing.

There's one place I am *not* allowed to go. That's their work lab in our basement. They do very secret work down there, and I am totally forbidden to go there unless they invite me.

Gates and I grabbed rolls of paper towels and began to wipe up the gooey egg yolk from everywhere. When we were finished, the kitchen looked almost normal, except for two yellow streaks down the wall.

"See you tomorrow. I'm sure we can fix Francine's programming," Gates said.

"We'd *better*!" I said. "No way we'll win the contest against Swanson Academy if all she does is smash eggs on people's heads."

Gates snickered. "It wasn't totally bad. We *did* give Chaz a good scare."

"This machine is dangerous," Mrs. Bernard said, waving her mop in the air. "It doesn't belong in the house."

Gates went home. Mom and Dad and I had spaghetti and meatballs for dinner. I talked about some kids at school. Mom and Dad talked about a bot they were programming that could answer riddles.

We didn't talk about Francine and the egg disaster.

But after dinner, my parents carried the robot down to their basement lab to examine it. I stayed in my room, trying to concentrate on my homework. But I was too eager to hear their report. I couldn't think straight.

They came upstairs after about an hour. I hurried down to the living room to hear their news.

Dad placed the robot against the mantelpiece. Mom waved a sheet of paper in front of her. I could see that it had lines of programming code on it.

"So?" I asked. "Did you find what's wrong with Francine?"

Dad squinted at me through his round eyeglasses. "What's wrong is the programming, Livvy," he said.

"Your robot was programmed to toss eggs and smash them on people," Mom said.

"No, we didn't do that!" I shouted. "Gates and I didn't program her to smash eggs. I swear!"

"Look at the code." Mom handed the paper to me. I blinked, struggling to read it.

"And look at the bottom," Mom said. "Look at the code. You programmed the robot to do that weird laugh."

"No . . ." I murmured. "That's impossible . . ."

I gazed over the computer code on the page.

"I swear Gates and I didn't program her to toss eggs and laugh," I insisted.

"Well, I don't think she programmed herself," Dad said. *"Did* she?"

I turned to stare at Francine, and I felt a chill of fear at the back of my neck.

"Program herself?" I murmured. "That's impossible—right?"

Did you ever have a dream and you knew you were dreaming the whole time, but you couldn't wake yourself up to get out of it?

That night I had one of my super-realistic dreams, as if I were watching in high def.

It started out with Francine stomping out of the garage. I wondered who had left the garage door open. I watched her from the bottom of the driveway as she began to pick up speed.

Her metal feet thundered over the pavement. Her steel-rod arms swung at her sides. Her thick body leaned forward, and she ran with a steady, mechanical rhythm.

I knew I should follow her. I knew I should catch the robot and tug her into the garage. But something held me back. Some powerful force held me in place.

Francine was halfway down the block, running full speed. My heart jumped a beat when something came whirring around the corner. Another robot!

The two robots crashed into each other with a deafening *clannng*—metal against metal. I let out a scream.

Instantly, they began pounding each another with their iron fists. The sound of their fight was like thunder, crash after booming crash.

I held my ears so tightly I couldn't hear my own scream.

I watched them battle and struggled to wake up to pull myself out of this nightmare. *Wake up, Livvy. Come on—wake up.*

Finally, I opened my eyes. Wide awake. I sat straight up.

The dream lingered in my mind. I tried to blink away the picture of the two robots battling so angrily.

I gasped when I heard a *thud*. Outside my bedroom door?

I held my breath and listened.

Another heavy *thud*. From the stairs. Someone slowly climbing the stairs to the second floor.

Thud.

I felt a chill roll down my back. The footsteps were heavy and metallic.

I remembered I was going to bring Francine out to the garage in the morning. So I'd left her by the kitchen door.

Thud.

I realized I was shaking. My hands were clenched into tight fists.

I turned and lowered my feet to the floor.

I heard one more heavy footstep. The floor-boards creaked.

Silence now.

Was I dreaming this?

I took a deep breath and tiptoed across the room to the door. My skin tingled with fear. I could feel the blood pulsing at my temples.

I grabbed the doorknob with one cold, wet hand. I twisted it. Pulled open the bedroom door—and screamed.

I stared into the dimly lit hallway. Francine stared back at me.

The robot stood erect, arms straight down at her sides. It took me a few seconds to catch my breath. *This isn't happening*, I told myself.

"How did you get up here?" I demanded. "Are you programming yourself?"

Of course, I didn't expect an answer.

I peered behind the robot. No one else in the hallway.

"This is getting creepy," I murmured.

I jumped as the robot tossed back her head and uttered her laugh again. *"Urk! Urk! Urk!"*

The sound must have awakened my parents. Their bedroom door swung open and they came bursting into the hall.

Mom was pulling her nightshirt down to her knees. Dad's pajamas were twisted from sleep and he stumbled and had to catch himself against the wall. His dark hair was matted over his forehead. He squinted without his glasses.

"What on earth—" Mom started.

"How did that robot get up here? Livvy, why are you up in the middle of the night? What was that scream we heard?" Mom barraged me with questions.

"I—I—I—" I stammered. "Francine woke me up," I finally choked out. "She . . . came upstairs on her own."

"Don't be ridiculous," Dad snapped.

Mom scowled at me. She likes her sleep. She hates waking up before morning. "Why are you lying to us?" she demanded.

"I'm not!" I cried. I shoved Francine to the side, away from the doorway. "Why would I want to lie to you?"

They both shrugged. Dad pushed his hair from in front of his eyes, but it fell right back.

"You two are the experts in artificial intelligence," I said. "You tell *me* how this happened."

Mom and Dad exchanged glances. "I know what's going on here," Mom said. "You and Gates have cooked this up. It's a little experiment. You two have a bet to see if you can freak us out."

"No way!" I shouted. "I—I didn't do this. I swear." I curled my hands into tight, angry fists. "Why don't you believe me?"

"Because I know it's a joke," Mom said.

Dad raised both hands to signal *halt*. "Let's get back to bed," he said. "Livvy, please take the robot down to the garage."

"And no more trying to freak us out," Mom added.

"But—but—" I sputtered angrily.

"Livvy, a simple robot like this cannot climb stairs," Mom said. "And cannot think on its own. Your father and I checked the programming, remember? We know what this robot can do."

I gritted my teeth and *grrrrrd* like an angry dog. But I knew it was pointless to argue any more. I wrapped an arm around Francine's waist and dragged her down the steps in the dark. Then I carried her into the garage, the concrete floor cold under my bare feet.

A few minutes later, I was back in bed. But I couldn't fall back to sleep. How *could* I?

The robot was doing things on her own. And my brilliant-scientist parents refused to believe me.

I tossed and turned and kept rolling onto one side, then the other. An hour or so later, I was finally drifting back to sleep—when a noise from outside startled me awake.

"Urk! Urk! Urk!"

That's when I knew I was definitely in trouble.

8

Two days later, Dad helped me bring Francine to school because we had a Robotics Club meeting scheduled at the end of the day. Coach Teague wanted everyone to show the progress they'd made on their bots.

We propped the bot up in the back seat just like a passenger. It felt a little weird fastening a seatbelt around her. But I wanted to make sure she was totally safe.

Gates met us at the side of the school and we carried Francine to a corner of the Art room. Everyone was supposed to store the bots there until the club meeting.

I kept thinking about Francine all day. I couldn't help but feel a little stressed. What if Gates and I started to show her off and she went berserk again?

Ellen, my teacher, kept watching me. (Ellen likes us to call her by her first name.) I guess she could tell that I was only half listening.

I kept thinking about how Gates and I had reprogrammed Francine's memory module. Did we get it right this time?

Ellen's voice broke into my thoughts. "What do *you* think, Livvy?"

"Uh . . . well . . ." I knew the class was talking about pollution in the ocean. But I didn't have a clue about what Ellen was asking me. "I'm not sure," I said. "I think I'm against it."

The class burst out laughing.

I knew I'd blown it.

Ellen laughed, too. She's small and really smart and appears too young to be a teacher. But she told us she's twenty-three. Her laugh sounds like a bird chirping. "Livvy, I asked you what your favorite ice cream flavor was," she said.

That gave everyone a chance to laugh at me some more. I turned and saw that Rosa Romero was laughing harder than anyone. Rosa is my enemy. I don't know how else to say it.

Gates and I never wanted an enemy. I mean, who wants *that*? But Rosa is usually bad news for both of us.

She just always tries to prove that she is better than us. She acts like the perfect person, especially around Ellen or Coach Teague. But she laughs at Gates and me and constantly puts us down and throws shade on everything we do or say.

Mainly, she's just mean. Not a bully or anything. Just mean-natured and nasty to us.

"Rocky Road," I told Ellen when everyone had stopped laughing.

"Try to pay attention to the discussion," Ellen said. "I could see your mind was somewhere else."

"Sorry," I muttered, feeling my face grow hot. I knew I was blushing.

Rosa snorted with glee.

I'll pay you back at the club meeting, I thought. *When our robot makes your robot look like a baby toy.*

On my way to the Robotics Club meeting after class, I tripped on the steps and scraped my knee against the railing. I guess I was a little tense. I really wanted Francine to wow Coach Teague and everyone else.

The meeting was in the Art room. The other members of the club were already there. Gates and DeAndre Marcus were talking in a corner.

Rosa was perched on a window ledge, running a hand through her long, perfectly wavy black hair as she talked to her project partner, Sara Blum. Sara and I had been best friends at Springdale Elementary. But she got into Rosa's crowd, and now we hardly ever see each other.

Francine stood in the corner where Gates and I had left her that morning. The other two bots were on a long art table in the center of the room.

The others were small, maybe a little bigger than a tissue box. Francine was the only big, person-sized robot. The other two looked like machines—not like humans.

Gates was still talking with DeAndre. I started over to him, but someone tapped me on the shoulder. "Is that thing yours?"

I turned to face Rosa. She had the usual smirk on her face and was pointing toward Francine in the corner.

"Hey to you, too," I said.

"Is that yours?" she repeated.

I nodded. "Yeah. Gates and mine."

Her smirk turned into a wide grin. "You've been watching old movies? Didn't anyone tell you bots don't look like that anymore?"

"We wanted to do something a little retro," I said.

She sneered. "Well . . . he's definitely retro."

"It's not a he. It's a she," I told her. "Her name is Francine."

Rosa laughed.

Sara, back at the windowsill, joined in. "My cousin's dog is named Francine," Sara said.

Rosa stared at me for a moment. She seemed to be thinking of a mean thing to say next. Finally, she said, "Do you really like Rocky Road?"

I nodded. "Yes. I do."

"Me too," Rosa said.

"You two are like *twins*," Sara said. She and Rosa laughed. It was sarcastic laughter.

"Okay, people, let's see what you've got." Coach Teague strode into the room. "Sorry I'm late. Let's get right to it. Show me your bots. Let's see how we're going to crush Swanson Academy this year."

Sara, Rosa, and DeAndre readied their projects on the table. Gates and I left Francine in the corner. She was so big and heavy, we decided we'd bring her over when it was our turn.

"DeAndre, would you like to go first?" Coach Teague asked.

DeAndre nodded and slid his bot to the center of the table. It was about the size of a shoe box. It had metal arms on each side with clawlike hands. DeAndre had stenciled the word *MonsterMaker* on one side.

DeAndre activated it, and a small square block slid up at one end of the top. It looked as if the bot was raising its head.

"What does your robot do?" Coach Teague asked.

"You'll see," DeAndre replied. He has a soft, whispery voice. It always sounds like he's telling you a secret.

Coach Teague chuckled. "You're keeping us in suspense."

We huddled around the table and watched. One end of DeAndre's robot popped open, and a tiny box slid out. The robot tilted and small pieces of metal poured out from the same opening. With a loud hum, the bot's slender arms moved into action. They began pressing the small metal items onto the sides of the tiny box.

"This is cool, DeAndre," Coach Teague said. "Tell us what we're seeing."

DeAndre kept his eyes on the bot, but a grin spread over his face. "My bot is constructing its own bot," he said.

He spoke in such a low whisper, I wasn't sure I'd heard correctly. But yes, I could see the bigger bot attaching magnetic arms on the sides of the tiny bot.

We all applauded. "That's a killer idea," Gates said, slapping DeAndre on the back.

"It's a winner," Coach Teague agreed. "How did you think of it?"

DeAndre shrugged. "Couldn't think of anything else."

More laughter.

This is why I love our Robotics Team. Everyone gets to use their brain in new ways. Building the bots is a real puzzle. But thinking them up is crazy fun.

Rosa and Sara presented their robot next. It was about the same size as DeAndre's robot, except it stood up on one end. Its arms were like rods. There were bolts at the elbows.

Sara carried a box of LEGO bricks to the table and dumped them out in front of the bot.

Rosa held the controller in one hand. She pushed a button to activate the bot, and it began to hum.

"Since we're doing construction bots," Rosa said. "Sara and I designed one that can build a tower."

She slid a lever on the controller. The robot moved forward and picked up a LEGO piece. She controlled the robot's actions with two sliding levers and a few buttons. We all watched in silence as the robot began to stack one block on top of another.

As the tower grew higher, the rods of the bot's arms grew longer. The robot stacked ten blocks perfectly without a drop or a mistake.

Everyone applauded, even Gates and me.

She and Sara bumped knuckles. Rosa had her eyes on me. It was like she was challenging me. *Go ahead, Livvy. Let's see you beat that.*

"Gates and Livvy, you go next," Coach Teague said. "I can't wait to see what that giant retro bot can do."

A wave of dread tightened my throat.

Gates and I had completely reprogrammed Francine. Did we get it right this time?

We carried our bot to the side of the table. I brought out a bowl of eggs we had stashed in the supply closet. And a small skillet. I set the bowl and skillet down in front of Francine.

"This is Francine," I announced.

Coach Teague chuckled. "We might want to rethink that name," he murmured. Everyone laughed. Rosa laughed the hardest.

"No. We like that name," I said.

Gates rolled his eyes. "Livvy likes the name," he said.

Oh, thanks for backing me up, Gates.

"We kept with the construction theme," Gates said. "We've programmed Francine to crack eggs and construct an omelet."

Coach Teague whistled. "Wow," he said. "Livvy, did your parents help you with the programming?"

"No way," I said. "Gates and I designed it ourselves."

"We had a few bugs the first time we tried it," Gates said. "And her parents helped us debug it."

"Livvy's parents are computer programming experts," Teague told everyone.

I wished he wouldn't talk about my parents. Gates and I did this on our own. My mom and dad would have helped. But we wanted to prove we could do it without them.

"Okay. Let's see Francine go," Teague said.

"Fingers crossed," I muttered, crossing them.

Please, Francine—no disasters like we had with Chaz in the kitchen. Please . . .

I nodded to Gates. He flipped the switch on Francine's back.

Everyone watched in silence. Watched and waited.

Nothing happened.

"Is it on a delay?" Coach Teague asked. "Did you check the circuits before you brought her in?"

"Worked perfectly last night," I muttered.

Gates flipped the power switch off, then on again.

We all watched in silence as Francine didn't move, didn't hum to life, didn't do anything.

Rosa was the first to laugh. "Guess we don't get to eat an omelet today."

"Stop it, Rosa," Teague snapped. "You know we're a team. We support one another, right?"

"Right," Rosa said, but you could see the total delight on her face.

Gates pulled open the control panel on Francine's back. He lifted out the battery pack. He shook it. "I brought fresh batteries just in case," he said. "They're in my locker." He set down the battery pack and disappeared into the hall.

Coach Teague had his eyes on me. "You tested the omelet-making before?"

I nodded. "We had problems, but then we fixed them."

No way I was going to tell him about Francine crushing eggs on our heads and heaving eggs all over the kitchen. For one thing, Rosa would enjoy the story too much.

Rosa and Sara walked away from the table and began to talk about their robot and how it was going to *kill* at the tournament against Swanson Academy. Coach Teague picked up DeAndre's bot and asked him some questions about the mechanics.

My head was pounding. Sometimes when I'm tense, I get these headaches. And trust me, I was waaay tense. The other bots were awesome, and I knew Francine could be awesome, too.

If only . . .

Finally, Gates came running back into the Art room. He had big drops of sweat running down his forehead, and he was breathing hard from running to his locker and back.

He slapped the fresh battery pack into Francine, and I closed her up. "Okay. Ready to try again," I announced.

Everyone returned to the table. Rosa and Sara were talking about a boy they both liked who transferred to Springdale last week. Sara said something funny, and they both cracked up laughing.

"Let's give Francine some attention," Coach

Teague scolded them. "We can't win unless we support each other, right?" he said again.

"We can't win if their robot doesn't even power up," Rosa said.

"That's not my idea of support," Teague told her. "Are we going to have to adjust your attitude module?"

It was a joke, but no one laughed.

I reached for Francine's power switch. "Here goes," I said. My heart felt like it was leaping into my throat. I threw the switch.

Everyone watched and waited.

Nothing happened.

Francine didn't move.

Then a very rude sound came out of her. *"Pppffffffftt."*

Everyone burst into wild laughter—everyone but Gates and me.

"Pffffffft."

She did it again.

The laughter rang off the Art room walls. Even Coach Teague was laughing his head off. Rosa and Sara slapped high fives.

When the laughter finally ended, I flipped the power switch on the robot a few more times. "I don't understand it," I murmured. "I really don't."

Rosa's blue eyes were dancing excitedly in her head. "Maybe you need your parents to help you with this one," she said, sneering.

Rosa knew just how to *get* me. She knew I didn't want to be compared to my parents. They are computer *geniuses*. I just want to do the best I can.

"If you'd like me to help you program it, I'd be happy to pitch in," Rosa said.

Gates and I knew she wasn't sincere. It was so obvious she said it to impress Coach Teague.

A great day for Rosa. A bad-luck day for Gates and me.

"It really did work when we tested it last night," I told the coach.

He shook his head. "Go back and get it right, Livvy. We can't enter your robot in the tournament if she doesn't work perfectly every time."

He turned to the others. "Congratulations on your good work. We have two robots that can definitely compete against anything Swanson throws at us. Now we just need one more." He waved to the door. "Let's meet again on Tuesday."

Sara and DeAndre picked up their bots and started to the door. Rosa flashed Gates and me one last triumphant smirk. Then she hurried after Sara.

"I don't get it," Gates muttered. "I just don't get it."

I stared at our robot for a long moment. *Something is definitely wrong here,* I told myself.

Is Francine doing this to us deliberately?

10

My mom picked Gates and me up at the side door to the school. We tossed Francine into the trunk of the car and drove to my house.

"I don't have to ask you how it went," Mom said. "I can see by your faces."

"Disaster," I muttered.

"Embarrassing disaster," Gates said, shaking his head.

"I think we need you to check out the programming again," I said. "Gates and I did something wrong."

"Not a problem," Mom said. "You may have just switched a few circuits in the memory pack."

I left Francine in the garage. Till after dinner. We had salad and then pepperoni pizza, and Mom and Dad carried on about one of their favorite conversations, "Are robots getting too smart?"

Mom thinks robots could be given enough intelligence to go out on their own and take over the world from humans. Dad thinks that scientists would never let that happen.

They never get tired of discussing this subject.

"I can tell you one thing," I interrupted when most of the pizza was gone. "Francine is not smart enough to take over for humans. She isn't smart enough to take over for a mosquito!"

Dad swallowed his last pepperoni. He started to stand up. "Go get her, Livvy. We'll take her down to the basement and check her programming again."

I hurried to the garage and dragged Francine inside through the kitchen door. Mrs. Bernard had started on the dinner dishes. She spun around as I shoved Francine through the door.

"Oh my, oh my," she said, wiping her hands quickly on a dish towel. "Do you have to bring that machine in the house?"

"It isn't on, Mrs. B.," I told her. "It can't do any harm."

She motioned to the kitchen walls. "Look at them, Livvy. Look. They're all stained. We couldn't get the yellow streaks off."

"I know," I replied softly. "But my parents—"

"That machine doesn't belong in the house. I'm not superstitious, but that thing is *evil*. I'm sure of it."

"My parents need to see it," I said. "I'm sorry. I'll keep it out of the kitchen. I'll be careful with it, Mrs. B. I promise."

45

She shook her dish towel at me, as if trying to wave me away. I couldn't hear what she was muttering under her breath as I dragged Francine through the kitchen and over to the basement door.

Mom and Dad carried the robot down to their basement lab. I told you, it's a Forbidden Zone. I'm not allowed in there unless they invite me and bring me down.

I went up to my room and tried to concentrate on my reading assignment. But I felt tense and totally distracted. So far, Francine was an embarrassing failure. And I needed to know why.

Mom and Dad knocked on my door less than an hour later. They walked into my room shaking their heads. They pushed Francine against the wall. Then they both dropped down on the edge of my bed.

I turned in my desk chair to face them. "So? What did you find?"

"Nothing," Dad said, scratching the back of his head.

My mouth dropped open. "Nothing? What do you mean nothing?"

"We didn't find any programming at all," Mom said. "The memory bank ... it seemed to have been drained."

I suddenly had a rock in the pit of my stomach. I gripped the top of my desk. "You mean—"

"There was no programming," Dad said. "No code. Nothing."

Mom squinted at me. "Do you think you and Gates could have accidentally deleted it?"

I gasped. "Huh? No way! How would we have done that?"

Dad shrugged. Mom bit her bottom lip. "It's mysterious," she murmured.

I jumped to my feet. "Mysterious? It's *impossible!*" I shouted. "Do you know how many hours Gates and I spent programming the robot? Then testing the program? Then programming some more?"

"Don't shout at us," Mom said. "We're just telling you what we found. The memory unit was empty."

"I—I—I—" I stammered. "I have to call Gates. Maybe he has an idea." I shook my head. "No, he won't. He'll be more horrified than *me!*"

Mom and Dad climbed to their feet. "You saved the program, right?" Dad asked. "You saved it on your laptop?"

I nodded.

"So it won't be too hard to put the program in again," he said.

"I guess," I muttered.

"Well, take it back out to the garage," Mom said, heading to the door. "It's freaking out Mrs. Bernard."

"And if you want your mom and me to help you reprogram it . . ." Dad started.

"No. Thanks. That would be cheating," I said.

"Gates and I will handle it." I sighed, and added, "I guess."

I listened to my parents walk down the stairs. Then I crossed the room to Francine. I put a hand on her shoulder. "Did you do it?" I asked. "Did you erase your memory circuits?"

Of course, the robot didn't move in any way. I suddenly felt stupid. *Am I going nutso? Why am I standing here asking questions to a mechanical robot?*

I slid my arm around the robot's waist and lifted her with one hand. I carried her out of my bedroom and down the hall to the stairs.

My brain was spinning. How did Francine's memory just vanish?

I suddenly had this wild idea. What if Rosa sneaked up to the Art room before the Robotics Club meeting and deleted Francine's program?

Possible?

No. No way.

I instantly felt bad even thinking that Rosa would do that.

For one thing, she wouldn't know which circuits to mess with. Also, that would be too dirty a trick for *anyone* to play, even Rosa.

I should be ashamed for thinking that.

Holding tightly onto Francine, I started down the stairs. I couldn't wait to call Gates. Would he have any clue at all about what happened?

I was on the fourth step down when Francine

suddenly moved. She kicked out one of her steel legs.

"Hey—!"

I let out a startled cry as I stumbled over her foot.

I couldn't stop myself. I toppled forward, tangled up with her leg, and went bouncing headfirst down the wooden stairs.

"Owwwwwwww!"

I screamed all the way down. Each step sent an explosion of pain down my body. The robot bounced on top of me, clanging at every impact.

I hit the bottom and sprawled there on my stomach with my arms outstretched. The robot bounced over me and rolled into the hall.

Stunned. I really did see stars. Red and yellow stars flashing and floating in front of me. I shut my eyes and waited for the pain to fade. But my whole body hurt so much, I had to force myself to breathe.

I heard running footsteps, and Mom appeared above me. "Oh no! Livvy—what happened? Are you okay?"

I groaned. "I don't know." I pulled myself up onto my knees.

Mom knelt beside me. She took me by the shoulders and helped pull me to my feet. "Is anything broken?"

I tested my arms and legs. I took a step. "No. I'm okay."

49

"Livvy—you fell all the way down?"

A burst of anger helped wash away my pain. "No!" I cried. I pointed a finger at Francine, on her side on the hallway floor. "No. No, Mom. She *tripped* me!"

Mom gasped. She still had hold of my shoulders. She turned me to face her. "Stop it, Livvy. You have to calm down. You're too wrapped up in this crazy idea that Francine can act on her own."

"She tripped me, Mom," I insisted. "I saw her. She stuck out her leg. Seriously. The leg shot out, and I fell over it."

Mom let go of me and took a step back. "You sure you're okay? Do we need to call Dr. Gurwin?"

"I'm okay," I said. "But do you believe me? *Do* you?"

"No," Mom said. "No, I don't believe the robot could trip you. For one thing, she has no memory, no programming at all. Now pick it up. I'll help you carry it to the garage."

All the pain was nearly gone, but I was *steaming.* Isn't it a parent's job to believe her daughter?

Okay, Mom, I thought. *Maybe you don't believe me now. But I know this robot is thinking on its own—and I'm going to prove it!*

SLAPPY HERE, EVERYONE.

Well, too bad, kids. Livvy and Gates aren't having much luck with Francine. Maybe they should melt her down and make a *can opener*! Hahahaha.

But I don't see the big fuss.

When Francine comes to life, she makes trouble for Livvy and Gates.

When I come to life, I make trouble for EVERYONE!

Well . . . if you think that you've seen big bot trouble, just wait. In a few chapters, *you'll* be screaming, "It's Alive! It's Alive!" Hahahaha.

11

Bright sunlight poured into the garage and made Francine glow as if she were on fire. Gates and I had her hooked up to my laptop, and we were feeding the memory program back into its module.

The robot's memory loss was still a mystery to both of us. Gates wasn't ready to believe that Francine had done it to herself. Of course, I had told him about how she tripped me and made me fall down the stairs.

He wasn't ready to believe that, either.

"Once we feed the code back into her, we can test her," Gates said. "You know. Get a bowl of eggs. Let her crack them."

Gates had his fingers crossed. "I have a good feeling about this," he said. "I'm not sure why. But I think this time, everything is going to work."

And that's when Rosa appeared in the open garage doorway. She had her silky black hair tied back in a single ponytail. She wore a white polo shirt and shorts. "Hey, guys." She greeted us as if we were the best of friends.

"Rosa? What's up?" Gates asked.

She stepped into the garage and crossed to Francine. "I thought maybe I could help," she said. She glanced at the laptop screen as the programming code was fed into the robot.

"You really want to help us?" I couldn't keep the surprise from my voice.

"We're a team, right?" Rosa replied. "I mean, Coach Teague says we should act like a team. And I know you two are in trouble with your robot."

"We're not exactly in trouble," I said. "We just have a few bugs to iron out."

Rosa picked up a screwdriver from the workbench and started to slap the blade against her hand. "You know, my LEGO-building robot is getting a lot of attention."

"Awesome," Gates said. But he didn't say it like he meant it.

"Some tech websites already want to write about it," Rosa said. "And maybe the toy company wants to buy it. Do you *believe* that?"

"Wow. That's terrific," I said. I didn't show any enthusiasm either.

I realized that Rosa didn't come over to help. She came here to brag.

She set the screwdriver back down on the table. "I'm thinking I might want a career in programming robots. I know I'd be good at it."

Gates and I were in no mood for her bragging. We had serious work to do on Francine. We had to test the new programming and make sure it would work this time.

"Maybe you should take your robot apart and start fresh," Rosa said.

Start over? I wanted to slug her. But I held myself back. "I don't think that's a good idea," I said.

Rosa saw that I was angry. "Just trying to think of everything," she said. "You know. I just put the idea out there."

Gates squinted at the laptop screen. "The program is loaded," he announced.

"Does that mean you're going to test her?" Rosa asked. "Can I watch?"

"I guess," I said.

Gates removed the laptop connecting cable from the robot. "Move Francine over here to the table," I said. "We'll do some simple tests first. Just to make sure we made the right connections."

"Fingers crossed," Rosa said, moving up beside me.

Gates reached for the robot. But Francine moved quickly. Her arms shot forward and her claws snapped around his waist.

"Nooooooo!" He screamed as the robot lifted him off the garage floor.

Francine raised him high above her head.

Gates squirmed and kicked and thrashed his arms. But the robot held on, gripping him tightly.

"Stop her! Stop her!" The scream burst from my throat.

I saw that Rosa was screaming, too, her hands pressed against her cheeks.

I dove toward the robot. Too late.

Francine raised Gates high over her head— and heaved him!

Heaved him hard. Sent him sailing out through the open garage door.

Rosa's shrill scream of horror rang in my ears.

Gasping for breath, I turned and watched Gates sail over the driveway. The robot's powerful heave sent him flying halfway down the drive.

And then with a cry of pain, he landed hard on his hands and knees. He rolled over once, then skidded, still screaming. And then the scream cut short and Gates didn't move.

"Livvy—watch out!"

Rosa's cry of warning came too late.

I felt Francine's claws dig into my waist.

"Nooo!" I pushed myself forward, dove to scramble away.

But the robot was too strong for me, her grip too tight.

My hands flew up helplessly as I felt myself being lifted off the garage floor.

"No! Let go! Let *go*!"

Rosa looked on, frozen in horror, her eyes bulging, hands still pressed to her cheeks.

"Let go! Let me go!"

I flailed wildly, kicking and twisting, as the robot shoved me high above her head. Pulled back her arms. And sent me soaring.

My scream must have rung out for miles as I went hurtling headfirst over the driveway.

12

I woke up screaming. My whole body was trembling. My nightshirt was drenched in sweat.

That was the most realistic dream I ever had.

I tried to blink the dream away. I could still feel myself sailing over the driveway.

Shivering, I lowered my feet to the floor. I gazed around my room, at the dark shadows shifting from the streetlight near the curb. Still night.

Somehow I expected Francine to be standing there, head tossed back, laughing her ugly laugh.

Maybe the dream was trying to tell me something, I thought. *Maybe Gates and I SHOULD take Francine apart.*

My head wouldn't stop spinning. The dream just wouldn't fade away.

The robot has only caused us trouble, I told myself. *And now it's giving me frightening nightmares.*

Gates and I could start all over, I decided. *There*

is still time to build something new. Especially if we do a smaller bot, a simpler bot.

Francine is too big. Too old-fashioned-looking. And we haven't been able to get the programming right. It has been a disaster.

Kids are laughing at us. Every time we fail with Francine it makes Rosa so happy.

And . . . I hadn't forgotten that Francine almost broke Chaz's wrist.

It's almost like she has an evil mind of her own. She deserves to be taken apart. Maybe we could use the memory modules to make . . .

Wait a minute.

A new idea broke into my thoughts.

I pictured Chaz. Chaz Fremont with his spiky red hair, his tiny blue eyes. That *I'm-so-hot* smirk on his face. Chaz thinking he's the king of all Robotics.

Suddenly, I knew what was going on. Suddenly, I knew why Francine was acting so badly. Suddenly, I knew whose fault the whole thing was.

I squinted at the clock on my bed table. Six thirty in the morning. I didn't care.

I grabbed my phone and punched in Gates's number.

"Hello?" I heard his scratchy voice after the fourth ring. "Livvy?"

"Listen to me, Gates," I said. "I figured the whole thing out."

"Huh? Figured *what* out?" He yawned.

"Wake up, will you?" I said. "I figured out our problem. With Francine."

"What time is it? It's still dark out, Livvy."

"Shut up and listen," I said. "I know exactly what we have to do."

13

After school the next day, Gates and I dragged Francine onto the North Springdale bus. The driver scratched his bald head and squinted at her. "Do you have a bus pass for her?" he asked.

"She's a robot," I said.

He shut the bus door and returned his hands to the wheel. "You need a city robot pass. They're half price this week."

"But—" I started.

He laughed. "I'm just messing with you."

Gates and I pretended we enjoyed his little joke. He waved us to the back, leaned over the wheel, and pulled the bus away from the curb. "Nice-looking thing," he called after us. "Where did you buy it?"

"We built it," Gates told him.

We dragged Francine to the back of the bus and sat down. Gates held one arm and I held the other. There were only two other passengers on the bus, and they both kept glancing suspiciously at Francine.

Chaz lives on the other side of town from us. The bus passed big houses with wide front lawns and tall hedges hiding them from the street. Teams of gardeners worked on some of the lawns. I pointed out the window as we passed one house with a four-car garage that was a lot bigger than my house.

"My cousin Ed goes to Swanson Academy," Gates said. "He says the kids are really nice."

"He probably doesn't know Chaz," I muttered.

We reached the stop near Chaz's house. Gates climbed down first and I tried to hand Francine to him. But I tripped on the step and the big robot toppled onto Gates. He stumbled back but managed to hold on to her.

"The next bot we build will be the size of a mouse," I promised.

We dragged Francine along the sidewalk. The air smelled sweet, of cut grass. A soft breeze made a tall willow tree shiver as we passed by. A little white dog yapped at us from a wide front porch.

We found Chaz at the top of his long, paved driveway. He was facing a basketball hoop over the double doors of his white-shingled garage.

On the driveway beside him, he had a bot that looked like an egg carton. It had long metal arms with big claws at the ends.

"Hey, Chaz," I called.

Startled, he spun around. His face instantly formed a scowl. I could tell he wasn't glad to see us.

"What's up?" Gates said. We pulled Francine over to him.

"What do you want?" Chaz demanded. He pointed at Francine. His face twisted in disgust. "Why did you bring that junk heap here? Don't you have a big enough garbage can to toss it in?"

"Nice to see you, too," I said sarcastically.

Chaz's little blue eyes flashed in his freckled face. "Did you come to apologize to me for what your robot did? Okay. Apology accepted. Now get lost."

Gates and I didn't reply. We both narrowed our eyes at Chaz.

"We know what you did," I said softly.

He blinked. "What *I* did?" He snickered. "What did I do?"

"You know," I said.

Gates stared hard at Chaz. "When you went to Livvy's house and took Francine from the garage . . . We know you hacked into the programming code."

"What kind of malware did you use, Chaz?" I demanded. "You infected Francine with some kind of virus. Admit it."

62

"That's sick," Chaz said, sneering. "You both have sick minds."

"Admit it," I repeated. "That day you showed up at my house, you did something to our bot. We know it was you."

Chaz ran a hand through his spiky red hair. He shook his head. "Why would I do that? Why would I bother with your piece of trash? My bot is so awesome . . ."

I glanced at the egg carton with arms on the driveway. What was so awesome about it?

"No way I'd hack into your stupid bot," Chaz insisted. "Watch how incredible my bot is. Just watch. Here's a lesson in genius bot-building."

He pulled a controller from his pocket and activated the little bot on the driveway. It began to hum and its long arms shot out in front of it.

Chaz picked up a little basketball from the driveway and placed it between the bot's clawed hands. Then he pushed another dial on the controller.

The bot tossed the ball up to the basket. It sank through the net with a perfect *swisssh* sound.

"Three points!" Chaz cried.

He ran after the ball and shoved it back into the bot's hands. "Again."

The bot tossed the ball up. This time it hit the rim and bounced off.

"That's okay," Chaz said, running after the ball. "No one is perfect."

He gave the bot another shot. The ball sailed high and dropped through the net.

"Three points!" Chaz shouted. He grabbed his regular-sized ball, spun around—and heaved it at Gates. "Think fast!"

The ball slammed into Gates's stomach. His eyes bulged as the air shot out of him, and he doubled over, struggling to catch his breath.

I scowled angrily at Chaz. "Why did you do that?"

He shrugged. "Beats me. I guess I don't like to be accused of things I didn't do."

"Well . . . somebody messed with Francine's programming," I said.

"Why would they bother?" Chaz replied. "You're not going to win any tournaments with a bot that looks like it's from a grandma movie."

Gates stood up tall. He was still breathing hard, holding his belly.

"Okay, okay," I said. "Maybe you didn't do it. Maybe I was wrong."

From the corner of my eye, I saw something move. It took me a few seconds to realize it was Francine. I had hit the remote by accident.

I spun around and gasped. And watched our tall bot begin to move forward. She took a hard, clomping step, her steel foot thudding on the driveway. Then another.

"Hey—what's going on?" Chaz cried. His eyes widened in alarm, and he took a step back.

"Francine—STOP!" I screamed.

But she raised her right leg high. Slammed it down hard. And *crushed* Chaz's bot beneath her heavy steel foot.

14

"I'm sorry we have to have this meeting," Coach Teague said. His eyes gazed around the room and then stopped at Gates and me.

We were in the gym, sitting on low stools he had brought into his office. My parents were there and so was Gates's mom. His dad was in Cleveland on a business trip.

"We're sorry, too," Dad said. "When we heard that Livvy's bot destroyed another bot, we were shocked. And upset."

Gates's mom had her hands clasped tightly in her lap. She is small and frail-looking, with the same dark hair and dark eyes as Gates. "But it was completely an accident, right?" she said. "I mean, it wasn't deliberate in any way?"

Coach Teague nodded. "We *think* it was an accident," he said, eyes still on me. "Even though the programming shows that the bot was set up to crush objects beneath its feet."

"Excuse me?" I jumped off my stool. "Gates and I—"

"Your parents ran the programming for us," Teague interrupted.

Mom shrugged. "I'm so sorry, dear. The bot was programmed to raise its foot and bring it down on any object beneath it. Your dad and I double checked the memory module."

"But—but—" I stammered, still on my feet. "Gates and I didn't program that. We would never—"

"Are we going to be suspended from school?" Gates interrupted.

Coach Teague shook his head. "No. I talked to the Robotics coach at Swanson Academy. He believes you when you say it was an accident. You and Livvy will not be suspended from school."

Gates let out a whoosh of air. He settled back on his stool.

"But your bot is disqualified," Teague continued. "Your bot will not be allowed to compete in the tournament."

I had a heavy feeling in the pit of my stomach. "Does that mean we're kicked off the Robotics Team?" I asked in a trembling voice.

"No. You can still be a part of it," Teague said. "You can help the others with their bots."

Oh, awesome sauce. I can help Rosa with her stupid block-building bot. Yay.

"What if Livvy and I design a whole new bot?" Gates asked.

Teague shook his head. "It's only a week till the tournament. Do you have any new ideas?"

"Not really," I said.

"Then just wait. You'll have a whole year to build something good for next year's tournament."

Next year?

Everyone could see how sad and upset Gates and I felt.

Gates's mom leaned forward on her stool and spoke up. "It seems like they are being punished for something they didn't do."

Coach Teague rubbed his chin, as if he was thinking hard about that. "It's true we don't know who programmed the bot to crush things. But Livvy and Gates carried the robot across town to Chaz Fremont's house and allowed the robot to crush his project."

"We need to solve the mystery of how the bot got programmed to do that," my dad chimed in. "As you know, Coach Teague, my wife and I are programming experts. And we work with artificial intelligence. When we get home, we'll take Francine apart and see if we can solve the mystery."

"I hope you can figure out what happened," Teague said.

"Gates and I spent months on the memory module, Dad," I said. "Do you have to take it apart?"

Mom answered for him. "I think that's the *first* thing we'll take apart to study. That's where the problem has to be."

Our parents and Coach Teague chatted some more, but I tuned out. Gates had his eyes on the floor. I felt kind of sick.

I mean, he and I aren't used to being in trouble. In fact, we're used to being the smart kids in our class, not losers who have to be punished.

I was glad when the meeting finally broke up. We walked out of the gym and down the hall. I could see the other members of our Robotics Team in the doorway of the Art room. Rosa had a big grin on her face.

I kept my eyes straight forward and acted as if I didn't see her.

"Did you two get suspended?" she called after us.

"No. Only our robot got suspended," I called back, and I kept walking.

In the school parking lot, my parents talked with Gates's mom in front of her car. Gates and I wandered to the fence and watched them.

"My mom doesn't know anything about computers or robots," Gates said. "She's totally confused by all this."

"We are *all* confused," I said.

"She thinks you and I deliberately did something wrong," Gates murmured. "She hated being called into school."

"Maybe my parents will figure it out," I said. "Why don't you come home with me. We can talk to my mom and dad about what they plan to do."

So, Gates and I rode home with my parents. It was a silent ride. No one spoke. Mom and Dad had their faraway thoughtful looks on their faces as they stared out the windshield.

Mrs. Bernard greeted us at the door. She had a long-handled mop in her hands. She scrunched up her face when Gates and I entered the house.

"I told you there was something wrong with that loopy machine," she said. "I knew it was going to get you into trouble."

I sighed. "Guess you were right, Mrs. B."

Gates and I grabbed juice boxes from the fridge. We gulped them down, then walked into the garage to say good-bye to Francine. The bot stood stiffly against the wall, arms limp at her sides, head down—as if she knew her fate.

"I thought this bot was going to be a winner," I said. "But we never even got her egg-cracking skill to work properly."

My throat tightened up. I almost felt like crying. We had both worked so hard . . .

"There is something going on we don't understand," Gates murmured.

And then Francine raised her head. Her steel mouth dropped open, and that annoying laugh came from somewhere inside her.

"Urk! Urk! Urrrk!"

I could feel the anger burst over my whole body. I let out an angry roar. I gripped both sides of the robot's head—*and ripped it off!*

Gates gasped.

Trembling with anger, I held the head in front of me. And the laughter didn't stop. It poured from the head in my hands.

"Urk! Urrrrk! Urrk! Urk! Urk!"

15

Gates clapped his hands over his ears. "Make it stop!" he screamed. "Smash it! Smash it!"

"Urk! Urk! Urk!"

"Are you crazy?" I cried. "If I smash it, we'll never find out what's making her do this."

Dad burst into the garage. "Hey—turn that laughing off," he shouted.

"I—I can't!" I stammered.

He grabbed the robot head from my hands. He gazed at the torn circuits under the chin. Then he shook the head as hard as he could.

"Urk! Urk! Urrrrrk."

The ugly sound finally faded.

"Weird," Dad said, staring at the robot head in his hands.

"She's alive! I know she is!" Gates cried.

Dad snickered. "I'm sure there's a better explanation, Gates."

"I know it's crazy," Gates said. "But I'm right. She's alive—even with her head off."

Dad shook his head. "I think we have to stick to science," he said. "We're not living in a sci-fi movie, you know?"

"I hope not." Mom's voice broke into the conversation. I turned and saw her in the kitchen doorway to the house. "Robots can be given a lot of intelligence these days. In some ways, they can even think for themselves. But they're not alive, Gates."

"Only in movies," Dad agreed.

"No one programmed her to laugh that ugly laugh," Gates insisted.

"We'll figure it out," Mom said. "Robots don't laugh on their own."

I didn't join in the conversation. Mainly because I didn't know what to think. Of course my parents would stick to science. They were scientists.

But I'd seen enough scary movies to know that sometimes creepy things can happen. Creepy things that can't be explained by science.

Dad handed the robot head to Mom. He grabbed the body around the middle. "It's been a long day for all of us," he said. "Why don't you kids find something to do? Something to take your minds off the robot mystery."

"And what are *you* going to do?" I asked.

Mom held the door open for Dad as he carried the robot body to the house. "We are going to take this thing apart and study every module

73

and circuit until we know what happened with her," she said.

"Can we watch?" I asked.

"No. Sorry," she replied. "Too many secret, delicate things in our lab. We can't have the lab contaminated, dear."

"Huh? Contaminated?" I cried. "Is *that* what you think of Gates and me? We're like germs? We'd contaminate your lab?"

Dad laughed. "Yes. We think of you as germs. Of course we do."

"Haha." I rolled my eyes.

"Just be patient," Mom said. "It's only going to take us an hour. An hour at the most. Then we'll come up and tell you what we found."

"You can be patient for an hour, can't you?" Dad said. He didn't wait for an answer. He disappeared into the house with Mom. The door closed behind them.

Gates and I looked at one another for a long moment. I sighed. "What should we do now?"

He shrugged. "I'm kind of hungry."

We went into the kitchen and got bags of chips and more juice boxes. Mrs. Bernard stopped us on our way to the den. "Don't make crumbs," she said. "I just cleaned in there."

"No worries. We're very neat chip-eaters," I told her.

She made a *hmmph* sound and disappeared into the kitchen.

In the den, we sprawled on the big green leather couch, and watched some shows about sharks attacking people. There were Shark Week reruns on the Discovery Channel, one of our favorite shows to watch.

Gates swallowed a mouthful of chips. I saw crumbs all over the couch cushion. He wasn't a neat chip eater, after all. "What would you do if you were a shark?" he asked.

"Bite Rosa Romero," I said. I didn't even have to think about it.

We both laughed.

"What time is it?" Gates asked.

I glanced at the wooden clock above the den mantel. "Six thirty."

"When did your parents take Francine downstairs? Shouldn't they be done by now?"

"Definitely," I said. "They've been down there a long time. They said it would only take an hour."

Gates climbed up from the couch, sending crumbs raining down on the carpet. "Do you think something went wrong?"

"What could go wrong?" I said. "They were just taking the robot apart."

"They promised they'd come up and tell us what they found," Gates said.

"Maybe we should check on them," I said. I led the way to the basement stairs. The door was closed, as always.

I gripped the doorknob, but Gates pulled me back.

"We can't go down there," he said. "Remember your family rule? You're not allowed in their lab unless they invite you down."

"But this is an emergency," I insisted.

His dark eyes burned into mine. "An emergency? I don't think so. I—"

"Let's go down there and see what's keeping them," I said. I wrapped my hand around the doorknob again. "What's the worst thing that could happen?"

"Well... you could be grounded for life," he said.

"No big deal," I said. I turned the knob and pulled open the door.

I poked my head in and peered down the steps. The wooden stairway was steep and narrow. A single light bulb on the wall provided the only light.

The air was hot in the stairwell. I held my breath and listened for my parents' voices. I could feel my heart start to beat a little faster. The only sound I heard was the loud hum of the air conditioner.

"Come on," Gates whispered, giving me a little push. "Lead the way. We'll just take a peek."

I stepped into the stairwell. The first wooden stair creaked under my shoe. I stopped and held my breath again.

Did Mom and Dad hear that?

No sound of anyone moving down there.

Leaning hard on the banister, I lowered myself to the next step. Then the next.

Right behind me, I could hear Gates breathing hard. He was nervous, too.

We were halfway down the steps. Still no voices. No sounds of anyone moving.

Should I call out to them?

I opened my mouth to shout, but changed my mind.

At the bottom of the stairs, my parents' lab is behind a glass wall. I could see that the glass door to the lab was closed.

The ceiling lights in the lab were bright, casting a glare over the glass. My parents like a lot of light when they work.

Gates and I were nearly down to the bottom of the stairs. I squinted into the bright light on the other side of the glass wall, waiting for my eyes to adjust.

And then my parents came into focus.

Dad was sitting in a straight-backed wooden chair. He had his back to us. Mom leaned over him, tugging at wires.

Wires?

Yes. I could see it so clearly. I didn't want to believe it, but I could see it. I clapped a hand tightly over my mouth to keep from screaming.

A square flap of skin was open just above the back of Dad's shoulders. And Mom was working on a thick tangle of wires that poked out of his neck.

SLAPPY HERE, EVERYONE . . .

Haha. Livvy's dad is a scientist. That means he has a real head on his shoulders. The question is: Is it a *human* head?

Is her dad really a robot?

Maybe that's why he puts AA batteries in his cornflakes!

Maybe that's why he shouts, "COMPUTER ERROR" every time she hugs him! Hahaha.

Livvy has a lot of questions to answer. Like: What should she buy him for Father's Day? A bottle of metal polish?

Hahahaha!

16

My breath caught in my throat. Behind me, I heard Gates gasp. He stumbled, bumped me hard, and we both nearly toppled down the last of the stairs.

I grabbed the banister and caught my balance. I opened my mouth to scream, but no sound came out.

Gates grabbed me and spun me around. He raised a finger to his lips. "Sssssshhh."

"Huh? Why?" I whispered.

"This is too weird," he whispered back. "If they see us . . . If they know we know . . ."

We both stared through the glass wall into the office. Mom continued to untangle the blue and yellow wires that hung out from Dad's neck.

This isn't happening, I thought. *This can't be real. My dad can't be a robot!*

Was this one of my super-realistic dreams?

I shut my eyes tight and tried to force myself

79

awake. But . . . I already was awake. I realized to my horror this was no dream.

I stood squinting at the wires bobbing from inside Dad. His head was down. He slumped stiffly forward. His back was turned, so I couldn't see if his eyes were open or closed.

Gates grabbed my arm. He motioned to the top of the stairs.

It took me a few seconds to get my legs to work. They were trembling so hard, I thought I might collapse to the floor.

I followed him to the top of the stairs, my brain tilting from side to side like a seesaw. We stumbled into the hallway. Gates silently pushed the door shut behind us.

We leaned against the wall, both of us struggling to catch our breath. I wiped sweat off my forehead with the back of my hand. "My dad . . ." I managed to choke out. "He . . . he's a robot."

"It can't be your dad," Gates said. "That doesn't make sense. Something weird is happening here."

I rolled my eyes. "Something weird? Do you *think* so?"

"We . . . have to make a plan," he said, still breathing hard. "Figure something out."

"Why didn't you let me shout to them?" I demanded. "Why didn't you let me tell them we saw them?"

"Because we don't know what they would do," Gates said. "What would they do to us? If we told them we know their secret ... what would they do?"

"But they're my parents!" I cried. "They—"

Gates shook his head. "No, they're not. Your dad isn't your dad. He's a robot. And your mom—"

"We don't know about my mom," I said. My whole body shuddered with dread. "What are you saying, Gates? Are you saying they could be dangerous? We could be in trouble if they find out we know their secret?"

He shrugged. "Beats me. I don't know. I don't know anything, Livvy. I just know that I'm totally freaked out. I just keep picturing those blue and yellow wires poking out from inside the Dad robot."

"We have to tell someone," I decided. "We can't deal with this on our own. We have to tell someone we can trust."

Gates narrowed his eyes at me. "But ... who?"

A crash from the kitchen made us both jump. I heard Mrs. Bernard mutter, "Oh, mercy."

"Mrs. Bernard!" I whispered. "We can tell her what we saw, Gates. She's known me since I was five. I know we can trust her."

Gates thought about it for a long moment. "Maybe she already knows what's up," he said. "Maybe she knows the truth about your dad."

"She'll tell us," I said. "She's the most honest person I know. She once found a five-dollar bill on the sidewalk. And she went from house to house till she found the person who dropped it."

We started to the kitchen. "Think she'll believe us?" he asked.

I shrugged. "We have no choice. We have to try."

I stepped into the kitchen—and cried out.

Mrs. Bernard was down on the floor, a wide puddle of blood in front of her.

17

"Oh no!" I cried. My legs went weak and my knees started to fold up.

Mrs. Bernard raised her head. "No worries," she said. "I dropped the ketchup bottle. Bit of a mess."

I saw broken bits of glass at her side. She was on her hands and knees, mopping up the ketchup puddle with a roll of paper towels.

"Are you two okay?" she asked, pausing for a moment. "Why did you scream like that, Livvy?"

"I—I thought—" I stammered.

"We thought it was blood," Gates said.

Mrs. B swiped up the last of the ketchup and climbed to her feet. "Blood? Heavenly days. What would make you think that? Why do you two look so pale and shaken?"

My breathing started to return to normal. "Can we talk to you?" I asked.

She dumped the ketchup-soaked paper towels

in the trash can under the sink. "Talk? Okay. First I have to vacuum up the glass."

Gates and I waited, watching her vacuum the same area about a hundred times. What a clean freak!

Finally, we led her to the kitchen counter and the three of us climbed onto tall stools. "Now what can I help you with?" she asked. "What is the problem?"

"The problem is my dad," I said. "He isn't my dad. He's a robot."

Mrs. B curled a hand behind one ear. "What is that? I don't think I heard you correctly."

"A robot," Gates chimed in. "Livvy and I went down to the basement lab. And we saw her parents. And . . ."

"And my dad is a robot," I said. "The back of his neck was open, and we saw all these wires sticking out from inside him."

"He was slumped in a chair," Gates continued. "And Livvy's mom was trying to untangle the wires that came out of him."

Mrs. B blinked once, and her face appeared to tighten up. Her features closed in on themselves. I couldn't read her expression at all.

"Please don't laugh at us," I said. "We're not making up a joke or anything. We saw it. So please don't laugh."

She patted the back of my hand. "I'm not going

to laugh," she said, her eyes locked on mine. "I promise. I won't laugh."

"But do you believe us?" I demanded.

She twisted on the kitchen stool to face me. "I've been working in this house for about seven years," she said. "And I've always suspected something funny was going on here."

Her answer surprised me. She'd always seemed perfectly happy here, washing the dishes, cleaning up, and taking care of us.

"I had my worries," she said. "Have mercy, I've had my worries. That secret lab in the basement. Your parents disappearing down there for hours. And no one allowed to see what they're doing . . ."

"A lot of scientists have labs at home," I said. "I never dreamed something weird was going on. How could I?"

"Well, what about all those machines?" Mrs. B demanded. "All of those robot machines or whatever they call them. In and out of the house, day and night. Good heavens. Those things moving and talking . . . as if they were alive."

I knew Mrs. B was superstitious about the robots. But now she seemed seriously terrified of them.

"Do you know anything about my dad?" I asked. "Do you know anything about what Gates and I saw? Is he . . . is he really a robot?"

She rubbed her nose for a long moment. "I can't say," she replied finally.

"You can't say?" I cried. "What does that mean? Is there something you're not telling us?"

"I can't say," she repeated. "What I mean is, I don't know. I suspected things. But he always seemed like a nice enough man. He's treated me very well. That time my sister got sick and I had to go to San Francisco for two weeks . . . He was very understanding and generous."

Didn't she understand me? Didn't she understand what Gates and I were telling her? Or was she deliberately not answering?

Finally, I couldn't take it any longer. I jumped down from the stool. "Is my dad a robot or not?" I screamed. "Yes or no? Is he a robot?"

Mrs. B's mouth dropped open.

I heard a cough.

I turned and saw my mom and dad standing in the kitchen doorway.

18

Mom's face was twisted into a scowl. She had her hands clasped tightly in front of her. Dad had a strange smile on his face, kind of dreamy, like he wasn't really tuned in to what was happening.

Mrs. B had a look of fear on her face. She took a step away from the kitchen counter. Her eyes moved from Mom to Dad, studying them.

"Uh . . . Did you hear me?" I stammered in a tiny voice.

Mom nodded. Dad's smile slowly faded.

I narrowed my eyes at him. I knew he wasn't my dad. I knew he was a robot. I'd seen the wires. How could I ever erase that picture from my mind?

"I . . . Gates and I saw . . ." I choked out.

"Saw what?" Dad asked, his face still blank. His eyes went wide, like he didn't understand.

"We saw the wires," Gates said. He stood gripping the back of a kitchen stool.

"Wires?" Dad repeated.

"Why are you so confused?" Mom asked. "You

both look terrified. What did you see that was so frightening?"

"You . . ." I said. My heart was pounding so hard, I couldn't get any words out. "You were fixing Dad."

Mom's mouth dropped open. "Fixing him? You're not making any sense, Livvy."

"Yes, I am," I insisted. "Gates and I . . . We wondered what was taking you so long. So we went downstairs."

"Against our rules," Dad chimed in.

"Yes. Against your rules," I said.

I glimpsed Mrs. B at the sink. She was squeezing a dish towel in her hands. I heard her mutter, "Trouble, trouble."

"Gates and I just wanted to see what was taking you so long," I continued. "That's why we went downstairs. And then we saw you. We saw Dad. His neck was open, and he had all these wires poking out."

Dad laughed. It was a strange laugh. Like it was forced. He laughed a little too hard.

Mom squinted at me. "Why are you making up these stories? Do you still have robots on the brain?"

"Gates saw it, too," I shouted. "It's not a joke! We saw it!"

Gates nodded. "I saw it," he muttered.

"Is Dad a robot?" I cried, my voice breaking with emotion.

They both laughed.

Mrs. Bernard shook her head, still rolling the dish towel in her hands. I thought she believed Gates and me. But now I couldn't tell.

"You've had a big disappointment with Francine," Mom said when she finally finished laughing. "I guess that's why you have robots on your brain."

"Maybe it was the light," Dad said. "It sounds weird. But maybe the light on the glass lab wall had a glare and made you think you were seeing me with my neck open."

Gates had been quiet. But now he took a step toward my parents. "There's one way we can find out the truth," he said in a low voice. He kept his eyes on me.

"What do you mean?" I said.

He motioned toward Dad. "Check out the back of his neck. See if he has a flap back there. See if his neck feels like a human neck."

Mom and Dad exchanged glances.

"Is there a problem with that?" I demanded.

They both shook their heads. "Of course not, dear. But it's very silly."

"It isn't really necessary, is it?" Dad said. "Livvy, you know us. You know we're your parents."

"It's necessary," I said.

Dad shrugged. He gave Mom another glance. "Okay. Go," he said.

He turned around so we could see the back of his neck. "I hope you don't have cold hands," he joked.

Only Mom laughed.

Gates and I stepped up behind him. Dad's curly, salt-and-pepper hair came part of the way down his neck. Under the kitchen light, his skin looked smooth and tight.

My hand trembled as I reached up and wrapped my fingers around his neck.

19

I pressed my hand over the back of Dad's neck. The skin was warm. I squeezed my fingers tighter. I could feel neck muscles, tendons. Not metal or wires.

"Can we pull down your collar?" Gates asked Dad.

"Why?" Mom asked.

"See if we can find the flap," Gates said. "The little door that opens up."

Mom rolled her eyes. "This is too weird. I'm really worried about you two. I think you've lost your minds."

"Go ahead," Dad said.

I rolled down his collar. I rubbed my hand over his neck, his shoulders, the top part of his back.

Perfectly smooth. He has a mole on his left shoulder. That was the only bump.

"No flap," I reported to Gates. "His skin is perfectly normal. He's not a robot."

"Well ... I'm glad we got *that* cleared up,"

Mom said. She strode to the stove, picked up the teakettle, and filled it with water from the sink. "Do you two want to check *my* neck, too? Make sure I'm Livvy's real mom?"

Gates and I didn't reply. I think we were both feeling numb. In shock. I mean, we knew what we saw. We *both* didn't dream it.

But now, here was my dad. Just my dad, not a robot.

And how could we explain it? My mind was totally blown.

"Well, I've lived to see a lot," Mrs. Bernard said. *What did that mean?*

"I'm going to my room," she announced. She finally dropped the dish towel on the counter. "Call me if you need me."

"We won't need you, Mrs. B," Mom said. "We're going out for dinner tonight." She turned to Gates. "Would you like to join us?"

"Uh . . . No, thanks," he stammered. "I don't think so. I'd better get home." He gave me a little wave as he hurried to the kitchen door. I could see that he was as shaken as I was.

Gates and I were so freaked out, we forgot to ask Mom and Dad what they discovered when they took Francine apart. I didn't remember about it until halfway through dinner.

We were at Dad's favorite restaurant, The House of Meatballs. Dad loves meatball heroes and meatballs and spaghetti and anything with meatballs.

Mom always laughs at him. "Why don't you just have meat?" she says. "Why does it have to be rolled in a ball?"

"Doesn't taste as good," he always says.

Luckily, they have fried chicken and other food on the menu. I'm not really into meatballs.

Dinner went okay. We talked about things at school and some stories about my crazy cousins who live across town. No one mentioned what happened in the basement. Mom and Dad didn't bring up the subject of how Gates and I thought Dad was a robot.

I was very grateful. I didn't want to talk about it. I needed to think about it by myself. I needed to figure out exactly what had happened, and I knew Mom and Dad would not be helpful.

But then Francine popped into my mind. And I realized Gates and I hadn't asked about her, even though that's what we'd spent hours waiting for.

"I almost forgot about Francine," I said, finishing my last French fry. "Tell me. You took the robot apart? What did you find?"

Mom swallowed a mouthful of her chicken. "Not much," she said.

"We took the robot apart piece by piece," Dad said. "Module by module. We examined every part of her."

"Of course, we spent most of our time on the memory module," Mom added.

I shoved my plate away. "And?"

Mom shrugged. "Not much to report. We couldn't find any reason for Francine to act the way she did."

"There was nothing in the program that would cause her to stomp on another bot," Dad added. "I mean, nothing at all."

"So she decided to do it on her own?" I asked.

"Not very likely," Mom said. "Not with that simple programming. There's no way the robot was smart enough to act on her own."

"And," Dad said, "no way the robot was smart enough to program herself."

"Then how do you explain it?" I demanded. "Francine crossed the driveway and stomped on Chaz's basketball bot. And I didn't tell her to do that or program it or anything."

"As far as your dad and I could tell," Mom said, "Francine had programming to crack open eggs and drop the yolks in a bowl. That's all."

"But she never did that," I said. "Not once. She did all these terrible things she wasn't programmed to do."

Mom and Dad stared at me. "Frankly, we're stumped," Dad said.

"We work with very sophisticated computers and bots," Mom continued. "If there was a flaw in Francine's memory program, we would have caught it. We took the robot apart piece by piece. But we didn't find anything. Not a single line of bad code."

I thought about it for a long moment. "So it's a total mystery?" I said finally.

Dad nodded. "A total mystery."

Little did I know that the mystery was just beginning.

20

The next day, Coach Teague held a meeting of the Robotics Club after school. Gates and I walked into the Art room and set down our backpacks. DeAndre Marcus, Sara Blum, and my old pal Rosa Romero were already gathered around a long table.

I took a seat on the bench across from Rosa. DeAndre plugged the power pack into his bot, and it began to hum. "I've made some improvements," he said in his whispery voice. "I speeded up the tempo. So now it can build its own bot in under a minute."

"Wow. Impressive," Rosa said. For some reason, she had her eyes on me, not DeAndre or his bot. "Your bot is going to *kill* at the tournament."

Coach Teague stepped into the room, pulling a maroon sweatshirt off. "So hot today," he muttered. He tossed it onto a chair and swept a hand over his hair to brush it into place.

"Sorry I'm late. Budget talks," he said, making his way to the table. "How is everyone today? Feeling stressed about the tournament? It's only a few days away, as I'm sure you all know."

We all murmured answers.

"Well, we have two awesome bots to go up against Swanson," he continued. "Of course, they have a much bigger Robotics Team than we do. But I think we have something to show them."

Gates and I exchanged glances. I wondered if he felt as awkward as I did. I mean, we were the only ones without a project.

Teague turned to us. It was as if he read my mind. "I know there's only a week left," he said. "But did you two come up with any new ideas?"

Gates shook his head. He kept his gaze down, staring at the table. "Not really."

"It's been a little weird at my house," I said. "I haven't been able to think about a new bot."

Suddenly, I was desperate to tell Teague the whole story. Tell him about what Gates and I saw in my basement. My dad with his neck open and wires poking out.

What would Teague think? That I was dreaming? That I was crazy? That I was just making it up to get attention since I didn't have a bot to show off?

I kept my mouth shut.

Teague patted me on the shoulder. "Well, of

course, you and Gates will be at the tournament as part of our team. Maybe you'll get some good ideas for *next* year's projects."

"Yeah. Maybe," I replied.

Gates just shook his head sadly.

"I have *lots* of good ideas," Rosa chimed in. "Maybe I could share some of my ideas with Gates and Livvy, since they don't have any."

Coach Teague smiled. "Yes," he said, "that's what Robotics is all about. Cooperatition."

I wondered: *If Gates and I strangled Rosa, would that be called cooperatition?*

But I smiled and didn't say anything.

So, we ran the two bots through their paces. Teague had a few suggestions for the LEGO-building bot built by Sara and Rosa. Nothing major.

DeAndre's bot ran perfectly. It built its own little bot in under a minute.

Coach Teague congratulated everyone again, and said we were ready to "kick butt" against Swanson. Then Rosa and DeAndre carefully packed up their bots, and we left the school.

Heavy clouds hung low in the sky, and the air had grown chilly and damp. The gray weather matched my mood perfectly as I started to walk home.

I had crossed Palm Place and was halfway down the next block when I heard running footsteps behind me. I turned to see Rosa waving to me, calling for me to wait up.

Her perfect long wavy hair flew behind her as she ran. Her blue eyes were wide. Her cheeks pink from running.

"Hi," she said breathlessly, coming up beside me.

"Hi," I said. I couldn't keep the surprise from my voice. Rosa had never wanted to walk with me before.

"I just wanted to say I'm sorry," she said, brushing her hair off one shoulder of her silky blue jacket.

I squinted at her. "Sorry?"

She nodded. "Sorry about what happened to your robot."

Was she serious? I saw the big grin on her face when Coach Teague said that Francine couldn't compete in the tournament.

"You didn't look sorry," I blurted out.

Her cheeks turned a little pinker. "I thought about it. A lot," she said. "You and Gates worked hard on that . . . thing. I know you did."

"Okay," I said. "Apology accepted." I stopped at the corner of Maple Avenue.

"I was serious about wanting to help you," Rosa said.

"Really?"

She nodded. Her perfectly round blue eyes flashed. She reached into her backpack. "I thought maybe you and Gates could use this."

She pulled out a paperback book with a bright

yellow cover and shoved it into my hand. "This might help," she said.

I turned the book over and read the title: *ROBOTICS FOR DUMMIES*.

I held the book up to her. "Seriously?"

"It looks like a joke," Rosa said. "But there are some really good project ideas in there."

She knew it was a joke. A cruel joke—on me. But somehow she kept a straight face and a sincere expression. Like she really wanted to help.

I'm not a violent person. But for the second time that afternoon, I thought of strangling her.

"Hey, thanks," I said, shoving it into my backpack. "Gates will like this."

She looked a little disappointed. I guessed she wanted a bigger reaction from me. Maybe I was supposed to get angry. Or cry. Or rip the stupid book to pieces.

"See you tomorrow," she said. She turned quickly and hurried away.

What a weird person she is, I thought. *I never did anything to her. It's like she was programmed to be mean.*

Dinner at our house was quiet that night. Mom and Dad seemed to have a lot on their minds. They didn't talk much at all.

They usually batter me with questions about my school day. But today there were no questions at all. Just "Pass the string beans" and "Could I have a little more macaroni, please?"

100

"We had a Robotics meeting after school," I said, just to break the awkward silence. "The club has two good bots to compete against Swanson next week."

Mom flashed me a pitying look. "Sorry about your bot, Livvy. I know you worked hard."

"Yeah," I muttered. "It's a shame, okay." Then I told my parents about Rosa. "She gave me a book called *ROBOTICS FOR DUMMIES*."

Mom laughed. Dad didn't. "Was that supposed to be a joke?" Dad asked.

"Uh . . . yeah."

"I'd like to see that book," Dad said. "See who wrote it. It may be someone I know."

"I'll take it out of my trash can for you," I told him.

After dinner, Dad and I washed the dishes. My parents were totally tech savvy, but they didn't own a dishwasher. Dad always washed and I dried. We never switched jobs.

Usually, we talked about music. Songs we liked. We'd even sing a little to each other. Dad likes eighties hair bands and old heavy metal stuff. He's always trying to convince me they were so much better than the stuff I listen to.

Tonight, for some reason, we didn't talk. The mood was totally strained in my house. I mean, both my parents were acting gloomy and quiet. I had no idea why.

Dad rinsed off a big carving knife and handed

it to me. I tried to grasp the handle, but it was slippery. It started to slide from my hand. I made a grab for it.

But the knife dropped and the big blade sliced right through the back of Dad's hand.

"*Nooo!* Sorry!" I cried.

Dad was sponging off a dinner plate. He didn't seem to notice.

I stared at the back of his hand. The blade had cut a two-inch line in the skin. Dad didn't seem to feel the pain.

"Hey, Dad—?" I started.

He handed me the dinner plate.

"Dad? Your hand?" I said.

I grabbed his hand and raised it so he would notice. Then I realized the hand wasn't bleeding. The cut appeared to be pretty deep. But no blood seeped out onto the skin.

"Dad?"

He finally lowered his gaze.

"Your hand is cut," I said. "But it isn't bleeding."

He nodded. He raised the cut hand to examine it better.

"Didn't you feel it?"

"Not really," he said.

"Dad, that's totally weird!" I exclaimed.

"Yeah. Weird," he murmured.

21

Dad went to bandage his hand. I finished the dishes without him. Then I made my way upstairs to my room to do homework.

I finished a section of my science notebook. Then I stopped and shut my eyes and thought about a lot of things.

Everything galloped past me, as if my thoughts were having a race. Again I saw Francine tossing eggs across the kitchen . . . stomping on Chaz Fremont's bot in his driveway . . . Dad with the wires dangling from inside his neck . . . Dad's cut hand with no blood coming out . . . Rosa . . .

"Whoa." I suddenly remembered I hadn't told Gates about the book Rosa gave me. I texted him. Then I called him.

He wasn't very impressed with Rosa's gift. "Don't think about it," Gates said. "It's just Rosa being Rosa."

He was right. I had bigger worries.

I tried to get to sleep. I was really tired, the kind

of tired where it's hard to move your arms, and even your hair hurts. Probably stress.

And the stress was keeping me awake. Because I couldn't get the picture of Dad with his cut hand out of my mind, Dad not even noticing that the knife blade had sliced him. Dad with the wires in his neck . . . Yikes.

True, when he came upstairs, there were no wires. He had no flap in the back of his neck. He was perfectly normal.

But I saw what I saw. And so far, no one had been able to explain it to me.

I sat up in bed with a thought pulsing in my mind.

I'm going down to the basement. Mom and Dad are asleep. I'm going down to their lab. I can sneak down. I can be silent.

With no one down there, I could explore. Maybe I could find some clues as to what the real story was. Something that would explain the horrifying things Gates and I had seen.

My thoughts raced even faster. My whole body tingled with the excitement of doing something forbidden, something sneaky.

I'm such a straight arrow. I try to be good. I never do anything dishonest or against the rules. But for the second time I had to go against my parents' wishes.

I had to sneak down to the lab and see what I could find.

I climbed out of bed and tiptoed across the rug

to my bedroom door. I took a deep breath. I felt as if an electric current were running through my body. My heart thudded rapidly in my chest.

I pulled open my bedroom door, poked my head into the dimly lit hall—and gasped.

I covered my mouth to keep from crying out in shock.

And, my whole body trembling, I stared at Francine . . . Francine all in one piece . . . standing outside the door.

22

"N-no—!" I stammered. "You—you can't be here. They took you apart. They dismantled you."

I heard a low hum inside the robot's chest, like a machine starting up. And a tinny voice came from somewhere inside her. "Listen to me."

"No!" I cried. "No! I'm dreaming this! My parents took you apart. Besides, you're not programmed to talk."

"Listen to me." The tinny metallic voice again.

"How did you get up here?" I cried. "What are you doing here?"

The robot didn't have a chance to answer.

My parents' bedroom door swung open, and the two of them staggered sleepily into the hall. "I . . . heard voices," Dad said, adjusting the top of his pajama pants.

Mom brushed her hair down with both hands. Then she clicked on the hall light. Yellow light poured over Francine and me. Mom and Dad were both blinking at us in disbelief.

"Livvy—why did you put her back together again?" Mom demanded.

"You went down to the basement again?" Dad said. "Haven't you learned your lesson?"

"I—I didn't," I managed to choke out. "I . . . opened my door and—"

"This is not acceptable," Dad said angrily. He stepped up to Francine, his eyes running up and down the robot, a frown on his face. "We have to have some rules, Livvy."

"Rules?" I cried. "Why are you talking about rules, Dad? You told me you took Francine apart. Remember? So how is she standing here?"

"She's standing here because you put her back together and brought her upstairs," Mom said.

"*I did NOT!*" I screamed. "You lied to me! Both of you. You said you dismantled the robot to study her."

"We *did* take her apart," Dad said. "We didn't lie."

"Piece by piece," Mom said.

She looked uncomfortable. Awkward. They both did. Like they weren't telling the truth. Or they were hiding something important.

I studied them both for a long moment. Mom had her arms crossed tightly in front of her nightshirt. Her hair had fallen over her forehead again, but she made no attempt to brush it back.

Dad had his fists clenched tensely at his sides. *Why won't they tell me the truth?*

107

I turned my gaze to Francine. The glass eyes gazed blankly at the wall. The hum that I'd heard before she started to talk had faded to silence.

Before she started to talk?

Yes. Francine had talked. She had repeated the same words: *"Listen to me."*

Was she trying to tell me something? If my parents hadn't come bursting out of their bedroom, would I have learned some of the things I was dying to know?

Too late now. Dad had Francine under one arm and was carrying her down the stairs. I knew he was returning her to the basement. The Forbidden Zone.

But I no longer cared about what was forbidden. I had to know the truth.

And that meant I had to go down to their precious lab and talk to Francine—and find out what the robot was so eager to tell me.

My chance came after school the next afternoon. No one was home. The house was empty. It was my time to learn some answers.

23

I made Gates come with me. He didn't really want to go back down to my parents' lab. The whole robot thing was freaking him out.

"I can't sleep at night," he told me as we walked to my house after school. "I'm having very real dreams, just like you. Terrible nightmares. I just want to forget about Francine, forget about what we saw down in your basement."

"But don't you want to know the truth?" I demanded.

He shook his head. "Not if the truth is too scary," he said.

So, okay. We were both scared. And we were both totally confused.

How had Francine put herself back together? How did she make her way up the stairs to my room? Why did Francine keep saying, *"Listen to me"*?

"I seriously think she was trying to warn me

about something," I told Gates. We started up my driveway.

"That's crazy," he said.

"What *isn't* crazy?" I demanded. "Ever since we built Francine, our lives have been crazy."

"So let's leave her in the basement," he murmured. "Let's pretend the whole thing never happened."

"I'm ignoring that," I said, opening the kitchen door. "I can't believe you would be such a coward."

"Coward? Me?" The word seemed to shock him.

The breakfast dishes were still on the table. The frying pan on the stove still had lumps of scrambled egg stuck to it.

"Where is Mrs. B?" I wondered. "She always cleans up right after breakfast."

"Do you have any Pop-Tarts?" Gates asked. "I'm kind of hungry. Don't your parents keep Pop-Tarts in the cabinet?"

"Forget the Pop-Tarts," I said, tossing my backpack onto the floor. "Come on, Gates. We have to get down to the basement before they get back. Sometimes they come home early."

"Can we have Pop-Tarts when we're finished down there?"

Gates was acting weird. I could tell he was frightened. That's why he was stalling. I don't even think he liked Pop-Tarts that much.

"Follow me," I whispered. "Let's check out their lab."

"Why are you whispering if no one is home?" Gates asked.

I shrugged. "Sorry. I guess maybe I'm a little scared, too."

I crossed to the basement stairway and pulled open the door. I clicked on the light and peered down the stairs. Warm in here. And silent. I could suddenly hear the blood pulsing at my temples.

"You go first," Gates said.

He didn't need to say it. I was already heading down, the wooden steps creaking under my shoes.

I was halfway to the basement when I realized the lights were on. A white glare poured into the stairwell.

I stopped.

"Do your parents always leave the lights on when they're away?" Gates asked in a soft, quiet voice.

"I don't know. I'm never allowed down here, remember?"

My heart was pounding hard now. My legs felt kind of rubbery. I took a deep breath. "Come on," I said. "Let's just do this."

I forced myself to take the rest of the stairs. I stepped onto the basement floor. And gazed through the glass walls into the brightly lit lab.

"Ohhhhhh." A moan escaped my throat.

I saw my dad first. Once again, he sat in the

111

straight-backed chair with his back to us. But his head . . . his head . . . his head . . .

His head wasn't on his shoulders. Tangles of green and yellow wires hung out of a hole between his shoulders. And his head was on a table across the room.

24

Gates stumbled into my back, and we both almost toppled over.

Mom was in the lab, too. She didn't see us. We watched her plug a thick white cable into Dad's back.

Then she reached a hand to the back of her neck, and opened a square flap of skin. She plugged the other end of the cable into her neck.

"Oh, wow," Gates murmured behind me. "Oh, wow. Oh, wow." He tugged my hand. "Let's go."

He started to the steps, but I tugged him back. "We can't go," I whispered. "I . . . I have to see what they're doing."

And that's when Mom turned and saw us.

Her eyes went wide and her hands flew up in the air in surprise. When she got over her shock, she waved us into the lab.

I pulled open the glass door and took a step inside. Gates stayed in the doorway.

I saw Francine in the far corner, against the

wall. When I entered, she said, *"Listen to me . . . Listen to me . . ."* in her metallic robot voice.

"Mom—" I started. "I . . . don't understand."

"You—you shouldn't be here," Mom stammered.

I stared at Dad's head, resting at an angle on the table across from us.

"TELL ME WHAT'S GOING ON!" I screamed.

"Go away," Mom said. "Just go away."

"TELL ME!" I insisted, waving my fists in the air. "TELL ME THE TRUTH!"

"You're . . . both robots?" Gates stammered.

"Listen to me," Francine uttered from the corner. *"Listen to me . . ."*

Mom stared at me blankly.

"You're not my parents," I said, my voice trembling. "Where are my parents?"

"No more questions!" a voice shouted. And Mrs. Bernard came striding in from the back room. Her round face was twisted in anger. Her cheeks were bright red.

"What are *you* doing down here?" I blurted out.

"Why did you come down here?" Mrs. B demanded, spitting the words angrily. "It's too soon. Too soon for you to know the truth. My bots need more time!"

25

My head began to spin. Nothing made sense. Mrs. B in the lab? Talking about *her* bots? I suddenly felt as if the world had fallen away from beneath my feet. And I was floating ... floating in a distant dream world.

Mrs. B stood there, glaring at Gates and me, tapping one foot on the floor.

I finally found my voice. "*Your* bots?" I cried. "This doesn't make any sense! What are you talking about?"

"You are ruining my experiment," she said. "These parent bots have been functioning perfectly. And now you've ruined everything."

"Parent bots? Your experiment?" I cried. "I thought you were a housekeeper. What are you really?"

"This is *my* artificial intelligence experiment," Mrs. B said. She crossed her arms in front of her and kept glaring and scowling at us as she talked.

"I've spent my whole life programming bots like your Mom and Dad bots. My entire life!"

"You're . . . you're a scientist?" Gates asked. I could see that he was as shocked and confused as I was.

"My whole life programming bots," she continued. "My whole life working on powerful memory modules. Look what I've done." She motioned to the Mom and Dad bots.

"I have given them free will," Mrs. B said. "They think on their own. They act and move on their own. They have their own thoughts. How brilliant is that? How brilliant am I?"

"But—but—" I sputtered. "If these are your bots . . . where are my *real* parents?"

She ignored my question. "Do you realize what I can do?" she said, her voice trembling with excitement. "Do you see what I did here? I made bots that could take the place of humans. Take the place of humans in *every way*!"

Her voice rose higher and higher as her excitement grew. "I made new parents for you. You had no idea they were my bots. That's because I programmed them perfectly and built them perfectly. Admit it! You had no idea."

She is crazy! I realized.

I gaped at her with my mouth hanging open. I didn't know what to say. And then, I had a flash. And I realized something else I hadn't figured out.

"Francine!" I cried. "*You* programmed Francine—didn't you? *You* are the one who programmed her to do all those terrible things. It wasn't Chaz. It was you."

"Of course it was me," she answered. A grin spread over her face.

"Every time we brought Francine down here for my parents to study her, you programmed her to do something terrible."

Mrs. B nodded. Her grin grew wider.

"But—why?" Gates demanded. "Why?"

Mrs. B's eyes flashed. "For fun," she said. "And . . . because I could. I could make her do anything. And so . . . Why not have a little fun with you and your simple little bot?"

"But where are my real parents?" I cried. "Tell me. Answer me. Where are they?"

Mrs. B jutted out her chin. She narrowed her eyes at Gates and me. "Enough," she said through gritted teeth. "Enough."

"Answer my question!" I shouted.

"You know too much," she said, lowering her voice. "You've both seen too much. You know things you shouldn't."

"But—" I started.

"So sorry you came down here. I was starting to like you. But now I have no choice. Now you must be destroyed."

26

Destroy us?

Does that mean Gates and I are robots, too?

I squeezed my arm hard. My skin was real, and the pain rode up to my shoulder. I raised a hand to my throat and felt my pulse beating.

No. We're real. We're people.

Mrs. B turned to the two parent bots. "Grab them. Don't let them get away. We must destroy them."

The headless Dad bot jumped to his feet. The Mom bot unplugged herself from the white cable and spun to us.

I froze for a moment, my fear keeping me in place. But then I lowered my head and forced my legs to move and started toward the basement steps. *GOT to get OUT of here!*

I was nearly to the stairs when I heard Gates shout.

I twirled around—and saw that the headless

Dad bot had grabbed one of his legs with both hands. Screaming, Gates struggled and squirmed. He tried to kick himself free but tumbled facedown to the floor.

I raised my eyes and saw the Mom bot coming after me.

No time to think. I knew I needed a weapon. I saw a long metal toolbox on the floor against the wall. I dove for it, grabbed it up in both hands— and slammed it into the headless Dad bot's belly.

The Dad bot bent over—and froze in place.

I pulled Gates to his feet and tugged him to the stairs. We scrambled up the steps with Mrs. B screaming behind us. "Stop them! Stop them! They've seen too much! Destroy them!"

Gasping for breath, I burst out the kitchen door. I could hear Gates close behind me. We ran across the backyard and ducked around the tall hedges that formed a wall along the side.

"What are we going to do?" Gates asked breathlessly, his chest heaving up and down. Big drops of sweat ran down his forehead. "They want to *kill* us."

"I . . . don't know," I confessed. "Where can we go? Who will help us?"

I jumped as the back door slammed behind the two bots and they came running fast toward the hedge. *How did they know we were here?*

Gates and I spun away and took off, running

across the neighbor's backyard. We ducked around a round rubber kiddie pool and leaped over a fallen tricycle. And kept running.

At the end of the block, we darted around the side of a shingled garage, pressed our backs against the wall, and struggled to breathe.

My side ached from running. My temples throbbed.

I reached into my jeans pocket and fumbled for my phone. I pulled it out, my hand shaking.

"What are you doing?" Gates asked.

"Calling 911," I told him, my voice hoarse, my throat painfully dry. "We need the police. They're the only ones who can help us."

"But they won't believe us," Gates said.

"They've *got* to," I replied.

"What are you going to say?" Gates demanded. "That your parents were replaced by bots and the bots want to kill you?"

"Exactly," I said.

Gates shuddered. "Good luck with that."

"They've got to believe me," I said, crossing my fingers. "They've *got* to."

I raised the phone and punched in 911.

27

"Emergency Services," the woman on the other end said. "Is this an emergency?"

"Y-yes," I stammered. "My name is Livvy Jones. I live at 248 Little Street. My friend and I—we need help. You see, my parents . . . my parents have been replaced by bots. And they're trying to kill us."

Silence at the other end. My hand was shaking so hard, I nearly dropped the phone.

The woman finally spoke up. "Did you know it's a crime to play a joke on the 911 emergency line? You could get in a lot of trouble."

"I'm *already* in a lot of trouble," I told her. "I didn't expect you to believe me. But they really are trying to kill my friend and me. It's not a joke. Please . . . please believe me."

Silence again.

"You sound very frightened," she said finally. "Are you an actress? Are you pulling a prank?"

121

"Please believe me. We really are in terrible danger."

"Okay. I'm sending a patrol car."

I let out a long whoosh of air. "Oh. Thank you. Thank you. You'll see. I'm telling the truth."

"Miss Jones," she said, "do you want to stay on the line until the officer arrives?"

I glanced around the side of the garage. No sign of the parents bots. "Uh . . . I think we're okay," I said. "We're hiding on the corner. We'll see the patrol car when it arrives."

And a minute later, I saw a black-and-white patrol car slow down as it made its way onto our block. No siren, but the blue and red lights on the roof of the car were flashing.

Gates and I left our hiding place and went running after the car, waving our hands over our heads and shouting.

A young officer in a black police uniform climbed out from behind the wheel. He had wavy blond hair falling out of his uniform cap and a blond mustache. He narrowed dark green eyes at us.

"I'm Sergeant Miller. Tell me the story again," he said. "I was on the next block, so I was able to come fast and—"

"They want to kill us!" Gates cried. "Livvy's parents. Only they're not her parents. They're robots. Robots with special intelligence."

He shut his eyes. "Please tell me you're joking."

"It's real," I insisted. "It sounds crazy, but it's

really happening. Mrs. Bernard is our house-keeper, only she isn't. She's some kind of computer scientist, and she built these bots that look like my parents. Only they want to kill us."

"Bots, huh?" Miller said, frowning. "You mean like in a sci-fi movie?"

"Only real," I said. "And dangerous. Gates and I—we really are in danger."

Miller adjusted the cap on his blond head. "Okay. Let's see," he said. "Which is your house?"

I pointed. Then I started to lead the way, but he held me back.

"Let me go first," he said. "You two stay behind me."

We followed him up our driveway. Sunlight covered the front window. I couldn't see inside.

We stepped onto the front stoop. Officer Miller raised his hand to knock on the front door. But the door was partly open.

"Hello?" he called.

He pushed the door open the rest of the way.

Gates and I followed him into the front entryway.

My legs began to tremble. My stomach tightened. I felt sick.

I peered into the living room—and let out a cry of shock.

28

The Dad bot sat on the living room couch, his feet up on the coffee table. He was smoking a pipe and had a magazine in his hands.

The Mom bot wore an apron over her jeans and top. She was at the stove, lowering a tray of cookies into the oven. Our kitchen and living room are one big room.

She turned when the three of us burst through the door and put on a sweet smile. "Oh. There you are," she said. "Did you come back to apologize?"

I made a choking sound. "Huh? Apologize?"

Her smile stayed frozen on her face. "Yes. Apologize for all those terrible names you called your father and me. Are you sorry we had that awful fight?"

"I—I—I—" I stammered.

Mom slid the cookies into the oven and closed the door. Dad put his magazine down and, sucking on his pipe, gazed at the police officer.

"Sorry to intrude," Miller said, pushing his cap back. "These kids reported—"

"Where did you find them?" Dad interrupted. "We had a stupid argument, and they ran out. We were so worried about them."

"But we knew they wouldn't go far," Mom said.

"Well . . . they told me a strange story about robots wanting to kill them," Miller said.

"Seriously?" Mom said, and laughed.

"They're into Robotics in school," Dad told Miller. "And they're always making up crazy stories about robots." He tapped his pipe with the palm of one hand. "I guess it's good they have such great imaginations."

"Can I offer you a cold drink?" Mom asked, crossing over to us.

"No, thank you," Miller said. He took a step back. "If this was just a family fight, I'd better get going."

"No!" I screamed, finally finding my voice. "No!"

"Livvy and I weren't lying," Gates said.

"You shouldn't call the police just because you're upset with your parents," Miller scolded. He took another step toward the front door.

"Don't go!" I cried. "Don't let them fool you. Here. I'll show you. I'll prove Gates and I weren't lying. These people aren't my parents. They're bots!"

And I dove at my mother, spun her around, grabbed her by the neck—and ripped open her neck flap.

29

Only there *was* no neck flap.

Only skin.

And muscles under the skin.

My mom uttered a cry and spun out of my grasp. "Livvy—what are you *doing*?" she howled.

I didn't let her get away. I reached for her neck again. The skin had reddened from where I tugged at it. I squeezed her neck. Perfectly normal.

Dad was on his feet now. "Livvy, why did you just attack your mother?" He said it calmly, not raising his voice. His eyes were on Officer Miller.

Dad stepped up to me and turned around. "Do you want to squeeze my neck, too? Are you trying to prove something?"

My heart pounding, I grabbed the back of his neck. No flap. I took his head in my hands and tried to twist it off. It turned with his neck. Everything perfectly normal.

"It's a trick!" I called to Officer Miller.

He tugged his uniform cap over his forehead. "I think you should sit down and have a nice long family discussion with your parents."

He turned and vanished out the door.

Gates and I stood staring at my parents. No one moved for the longest moment. I heard the patrol car roar away. I kept my eyes on Mom, then Dad.

What happens next?

I didn't have to wait long.

Mrs. Bernard marched in from the den. She pointed to Gates and me. "They almost gave us away," she told Mom and Dad. "Finish them off now—before there's more trouble."

30

"I—I don't get it," Gates said. "Are they bots or not?"

No time to answer that question. My two parents came at us fast.

I tried to run. But I stumbled over Gates's shoes and fell heavily to the floor.

Dad grabbed me by both arms and tugged me to my feet.

"No! Please!" I cried. "Don't hurt me!"

His eyes were wide. His mouth was twisted in anger. He uttered low growls with every breath.

"Finish her!" Mrs. B called. "Finish her!"

And then I saw something. A little white disc. It was stuck deep in Dad's ear.

He grasped my shoulders and started to shake me furiously. But I freed one hand and reached it up . . . up . . . up to his ear.

And I tugged out the white disc.

Dad's hands slowly loosened. His arms lowered. He blinked at me, confused. "Livvy?" he cried.

"Livvy?" He squinted at me as if he didn't recognize me. "Livvy? Are you okay?"

He wrapped his arms around me and hugged me tightly. "Oh, Livvy. I'm so sorry."

But then he turned. Mom and Gates were struggling across the room. Mom had Gates by the shoulders and was slamming his back against the wall.

Dad let go of me and tore across the room. He spun my mother around—and pulled the white disc from her ear.

Mom made a whimpering sound. She blinked her eyes really fast. Then she squinted around the room. "Is everyone okay?" she asked. "Are we okay again?"

She patted Gates's shoulder. "What is happening? Was there some kind of fight?"

"We're back," Dad said. "We're back in control again."

"No, you're not!" Mrs. B shouted, moving toward us. She raised a slender black controller. It looked like a TV remote.

"Not so fast!" she cried. "I'm still in control of you. You can't—"

My dad dove forward. He grabbed her head with both hands—and ripped it off her body.

Wires and circuit boards spilled out from Mrs. B's open neck. Her glasses bounced on the rug. She stood upright for a few seconds, then tumbled in a heap to the floor.

"She's a bot!" Gates cried.

"A very dangerous bot," Mom told him. "We created her, but we didn't know what we were doing. We gave her too much intelligence, too much power. And she worked out a way to control us."

"She took over," Dad said, shaking his head angrily. "And she used these discs to do it." He took the white disc and heaved it across the room. "And that wasn't enough for her. She had to build copies of us so that she could control them, too!"

Mom rushed over to hug me. "We're so sorry," she said. "We lost control of our own creation. And it almost destroyed our family."

"And me!" Gates reminded her.

"And you," she said. She hugged him, too.

"But . . . what about the Mom and Dad bots?" I asked. "Where are they?"

"In the basement," Dad replied. "But they aren't a problem anymore. Mrs. Bernard built them. And they cannot operate unless she is operating. Good-bye, Mrs. B. Good-bye, Mrs. B's two bots."

"We'll show you," Mom said. "Come see with your own eyes."

We all trooped down to the basement. Sure enough, the Mom and Dad bots were hunched over, lifeless.

"They're not dangerous anymore," Mom said.

"But we're not going to destroy them. We're going to study them. They are very advanced, and we need to see their programming."

I swallowed. I was starting to feel more normal. Gates definitely looked calmer, too. He even had a smile on his face, staring at the lifeless bots.

Then I heard a tinny voice and raised my eyes to the other end of the room. Francine stood with her back to the wall, arms at her sides.

"Listen to me," she said. *"Listen to me."*

31

That Saturday, the Robotics tournament against Swanson Academy was just as exciting as Gates and I hoped it would be. It was held in the Swanson gym. And the bleachers were packed with kids from our school and theirs, cheering on their bots.

Gates and I agreed that Coach Teague had to be the nicest guy on the planet Earth. We explained to him that Francine wasn't dangerous any longer, that my parents had helped us totally reprogram her.

He thought about it for a moment, then he said, "Okay. You can compete. If that is all true, you can enter Francine in the tournament."

So there we were. And I couldn't describe how excited Gates and I were to be there. We had tested Francine over and over, and she had the egg-cracking thing down perfectly.

What a winner!

The Swanson bots were amazing, but we knew our bot was amazing, too.

We watched Chaz Fremont put his basketball-shooting bot through its paces. The little bot put up shot after shot at the basketball hoop. It made them all, and the crowd went wild.

Chaz was so pumped, he actually took a bow.

Our turn next.

Gates and I moved Francine to the center of the gym floor. The crowd grew quiet. Because Francine was so old-fashioned looking, she towered over all the other bots.

We set up a small table and a bowl full of eggs. Gates took the microphone to announce what Francine was about to do.

But before he could speak, Francine took a big step away from us.

"Hey, wait—" I cried.

I watched in horror as Francine moved quickly across the floor. She tromped to where the Swanson team had lined up their bots. Then she raised a big, heavy foot, slammed it down hard—and smashed Chaz's bot flat.

Horrified cries rang out. Angry shouts.

Francine backed away from the crushed bot and raised both claw hands high above her head for silence.

"I've locked all the doors," she announced. *"I'm in charge now. Listen to me. Listen to me carefully—and NO ONE WILL GET HURT!"*

EPILOGUE FROM SLAPPY

Hahahaha!

I guess Francine won the contest! She was a *smash* hit!

Now it appears the kids are ALL losers.

There's a lesson here for everyone: Humans can never win.

I mean, how can any human win over a smart robot? Or a brilliant dummy? You know, my IQ is so high, I need to climb a ladder to read it!

I'm almost as smart as I am good-looking! Hahahaha.

And speaking of looking, I'll be looking for *you* next time when I return with another *Goosebumps SlappyWorld* book.

Remember, this is *SlappyWorld*.

You only *scream* in it!

About the Author

R.L. Stine's books are read all over the world. So far, his books have sold more than 300 million copies, making him one of the most popular children's authors in history. Besides Goosebumps, R.L. Stine has written the teen series Fear Street and the funny series Rotten School, as well as the Mostly Ghostly series, The Nightmare Room series, and the two-book thriller *Dangerous Girls*. R.L. Stine lives in New York with his wife, Jane, and Minnie, his King Charles spaniel. You can learn more about him at RLStine.com.

See where it all began in
SLAPPYWORLD #1:
SLAPPY BIRTHDAY TO YOU

SLAPPY HERE, EVERYONE.

Welcome to My World.

Yes, it's *SlappyWorld*—you're only *screaming* in it! Hahaha.

Readers Beware: Don't call me a dummy, Dummy. I'm so wonderful, I wish I could *kiss* myself!

(But, hey, I might get splinters!)

I'm so great, I give myself *goosebumps*. Do you know the only thing in the world that's almost as handsome as my face? That's right—my face in a mirror! Haha.

I'm good looking—and I'm generous, too. I like to share. Mainly, I like to share frightening stories to give you chills—and make you do the Slappy Dance.

Do you know how to do the Slappy Dance?

That's right—you shake all over! Hahaha!

The story you are about to read is one of the most *awesome* stories ever told. That's because it's about ME! Haha.

And it's about a boy named Ian Barker. It's Ian's birthday and, guess what? He's having a party. At the party, Ian gets a present he thinks he's going to love.

Wouldn't you know it? The gift turns out to be a bit of a nightmare! Isn't that a *scream*?

Sure, it's Ian's birthday—but *I'm* the one who takes the cake! Hahaha!

Go ahead, readers. Start the story. I call it ***Slappy Birthday to You***!

It's just one more terrifying tale from SlappyWorld!

1

On Ian Barker's twelfth birthday, he received a gift that brought pain and terror to him and his entire family.

But let's not get ahead of ourselves.

Let's try to enjoy Ian's birthday for as long as we can. Just keep in mind that it was not the birthday Ian had hoped for. In fact, it quickly became a day he would have given anything to forget.

Ian came down to breakfast on that sunny spring morning, eager for his special day to begin. Almost at once, he had trouble with his nine-year-old sister, Molly. But that was nothing new. If you ask Ian, "How do you spell *Molly*?" He'll answer, "T-R-O-U-B-L-E."

Since blueberry pancakes were Ian's favorite, Mrs. Barker had a tall stack of them on the table. Ian and Molly ate peacefully for a while. Molly liked her pancakes drowned in maple syrup, and she used up most of the syrup before Ian had a chance. But Ian didn't complain. He was determined to be cheerful on his birthday.

But then they came down to the last pancake on the platter. When they both stabbed a fork into it, that's when the t-r-o-u-b-l-e began.

"Mine," Ian said. "You've already had six."

"But I saw it first," Molly insisted. She kept her fork poking into her side of the pancake.

"It's my birthday," Ian reminded her. "I should get what I want today."

"You *always* think you should get what you want," Molly declared. Molly has wavy red hair and blue eyes, and when she gets into an argument about pancakes—or anything else—her pale, lightly freckled cheeks turn bright pink.

Their mom turned from the kitchen counter. She had been arranging cupcakes on a tray for Ian's birthday party. "Fighting again?"

"We're not fighting," Molly said. "We're *disputing.*"

"Oooh, big word," Ian said, rolling his eyes. "I'm so totally impressed."

They both kept their forks in the last remaining pancake.

"You're a jerk," Molly said. "I know you know that word."

"Don't call Ian names on his birthday," Mrs. Barker said. "Wait till tomorrow." She had a good sense of humor. Sometimes the kids appreciated it. Sometimes they didn't. "Why don't you split the pancake in two?" she suggested.

"Good idea," Ian said. He used his fork to divide the pancake into two pieces.

"No fair!" Molly cried. "Your half is twice as big as mine."

Ian laughed and gobbled up his half before Molly could do anything about it.

Molly frowned at her brother. "Don't you know how to eat, slob? You have syrup on your chin."

Ian raised the syrup bottle. "How would you like it in your hair?"

Mrs. Barker turned away from the cupcakes and stepped up to the table. "Stop," she said. "Breakfast is over." She took the syrup bottle from Ian's hand. "You're twelve now. You really have to stop all the fighting."

"But—" Ian started.

She squeezed Ian's shoulder. "Your cousins are coming for your party. I want you to be extra nice to them and don't pick fights the way you always do."

Ian groaned. "Vinny and Jonny? They always start it."

"Ian always starts it," Molly chimed in.

"Shut up!" Ian cried.

"Just listen to me," Mrs. Barker pleaded. "I want you to be nice to your cousins. You know their parents have been going through a tough time. Uncle Donny is still out of work. And Aunt Marie is getting over that operation."

"Could I have a cupcake now?" Molly asked.

Ian slapped the table. "If she has one, I want one, too."

"Have you heard a word I said?" their mom demanded.

"I swear I won't start any fights with Jonny and Vinny," Ian said. He raised his right hand, as if swearing an oath. Then he stood up from his seat and started toward the cupcake tray.

"Hands off," Mrs. Barker said. "Go get your dad, Ian. Tell him the guests will be arriving soon."

"Where is he?" Ian asked.

"In his workshop," his mom answered. "Where else?"

"Where else?" Molly mimicked.

Ian walked down the back hall to the door to the basement. He thought about Jonny and Vinny.

Jonny and Vinny lived just a few blocks away. Jonny was twelve and Vinny was eleven, but they looked like twins. They were both big bruisers. Tough guys, big for their age, loud and grabby, with pudgy, round heads, short-cropped blond hair, and upturned pig noses.

At least, that's how Ian described them. The kind of guys who were always bumping up against people and each other, always giggling, always grinning about something mean. Mean guys.

"They're just jealous of you." That's what Mrs. Barker always told Ian. "They're your only cousins, so you have to be nice to them."

Ian opened the basement door and went down the stairs two at a time. The air grew warmer as he reached the basement, and it smelled of glue.

Under bright white ceiling lights, his father stood hunched over his long worktable. He turned as Ian approached. "Oh, hi, Ian."

"Hey, Dad," Ian started. "Mom says—"

"Here's a birthday surprise for you," Mr. Barker said. He reached both hands to his face, plucked out his eyes, and held them up to Ian.

Catch the MOST WANTED Goosebumps® villains UNDEAD OR ALIVE!

SPECIAL EDITIONS

JACK BLACK

Goosebumps

BLU-RAY™ + DVD + DIGITAL HD

JACK BLACK

Goosebumps

"A frightfully fun flick for families."
-Peter Martin, *Twitchfilm.com*

Now on Blu-ray™, DVD & Digital

The Original Bone-Chilling Series

—with Exclusive Author Interviews!

R. L. Stine's Fright Fest!
Now with Splat Stats and More!

Goosebumps — The WEREWOLF of FEVER SWAMP — R·L·STINE — SCHOLASTIC

Goosebumps — A NIGHT in TERROR TOWER — R·L·STINE — SCHOLASTIC

Goosebumps — WELCOME to DEAD HOUSE — R·L·STINE — SCHOLASTIC

Goosebumps — WELCOME to CAMP NIGHTMARE — R·L·STINE — SCHOLASTIC

Goosebumps — GHOST BEACH — R·L·STINE — SCHOLASTIC

Goosebumps — The SCARECROW WALKS at MIDNIGHT — R·L·STINE — SCHOLASTIC

Goosebumps — YOU CAN'T SCARE ME! — R·L·STINE — SCHOLASTIC

Goosebumps — RETURN OF THE MUMMY — R·L·STINE — SCHOLASTIC

Goosebumps — REVENGE of the LAWN GNOMES — R·L·STINE — SCHOLASTIC

Goosebumps — PHANTOM OF THE AUDITORIUM — R·L·STINE — SCHOLASTIC

Goosebumps — VAMPIRE BREATH — R·L·STINE — SCHOLASTIC

Goosebumps — STAY OUT of the BASEMENT — R·L·STINE — SCHOLASTIC

SCHOLASTIC Read them all!

www.scholastic.com/goosebumps

GBCL22

THE ORIGINAL Goosebumps® BOOKS
WITH AN ALL-NEW LOOK!

R.L. Stine's Biography

DOUBLE THE FRIGHT
ALL AT ONE SITE
www.scholastic.com/goosebumps

FIENDS OF GOOSEBUMPS &
GOOSEBUMPS HORRORLAND CAN:

- PLAY GHOULISH GAMES!
- CHAT WITH FELLOW FAN-ATICS!
- WATCH CLIPS FROM SPINE-TINGLING DVDs!
- EXPLORE CLASSIC BOOKS AND NEW TERROR-IFIC TITLES!
- CHECK OUT THE GOOSEBUMPS HORRORLAND VIDEO GAME!
- GET GOOSEBUMPS PHOTOSHOCK FOR THE IPHONE™ OR IPOD TOUCH®!

◼ SCHOLASTIC

GBWEB